A Prophecies of Angels and
Demons Novella

PARABLE

Book 3.5

CASSANDRA ASTON

CONTENTS

CONTENT & TRIGGER WARNINGS

This book is a work of fiction. No part of this book should be construed as true or accurate; no people or animals were harmed in the creation of this story. Parable is intended for mature readers and is recommended for 18+. Mature content and triggers are listed below.

Descriptions of torture and death

Allusions to rape and other acts of sexual deviance

Open door spice

Biting and blood

References to witches, angels, demons and other fantastical creatures

Explicit language

Mental and physical issues described

Please use caution when reading.

You're still here? No complaints then, you deserve this.

BOOKS BY CASSANDRA ASTON

Prophecies of Angels and Demons

Grave Secrets – book 1
Firefly – Simon's Novella – book 1.5
Grave Prophecies – book 2
Light – Gabriel's Novella – book 2.5
Grave Revelations – book 3
Parable – Peter's Novella – book 3.5
Fated – Sanura's Kindle Vella

Deadly Fae Duology

Whispers Among Thorns – Coming June 2025
Book 2 – Coming December 2025

Vicious Villains: A Twisted Fairytale Reimagining Anthology Series

Book 1 – Coming 2026

PROLOGUE

Helena

Helena felt it before it happened. That static place she'd been in for some immeasurable period suddenly bloomed to life. It unfurled into awareness, then sensation. A weighted heaviness that rooted her to the earth, centering her on one plane. Finally, blinding light as new eyes opened, and she turned.

Nothing mattered but the sight before her—her soul's reason for existence, her universe.

She ran, crashing into him and he caught her, mouth melding with hers as they reunited in one beautiful moment. They were hands, lips, bodies pressing closer, desiring nothing more than to consume each other—to become whole.

When they did, saying the sacred words that bound them together, Helena felt the rightness of it and knew no matter what she endured from now until the end of eternity, she could face it with Aniel by her side.

Hand in hand, they traversed a glittering rainbow of light refracting every known and unknown color of the universe. Winding down a steep slope, neither slipped nor lost their way until their feet set down on solid ground. Helena spun in a circle, wide-eyed.

"Where are we, my love?"

"This place is called Colorado." Aniel squeezed their laced fingers tightly. *We cannot go to Athens, my dove. It no longer exists.*

There was a momentary heaviness in Helena's chest, but it was chased swiftly away by the pulse of their soul filling her to bursting and she smiled up at him. "I will live wherever you are and wherever you are shall be home."

His lips tipped up as he leaned down to kiss her forehead.

"Helena?"

She pulled back from Aniel's touch and stared up at a man at least a hand taller than her. "Yes?"

"Helena, it's me, Aesop."

Helena's hand tugged free from her mate's as she let out a small cry and ran to him, wrapping him in a tight embrace. "But you're a man now!" His stoic expression never faltered as she released him, leaning back to take him in. "You are so tall. Taller than Georgios. Taller even than Lysander, I think. Where are they? And Mother? Are they here?"

Aesop's brows slid low, bunching at the center. "No."

"Why ever not? Isn't this the end of the world? I thought..." She trailed off, glancing to Aniel who wore the same somber expression her brother did. "Were they..."

"They were not welcome in Alaxia, my dove."

A sob bubbled up Helena's chest. Her mother had been kind and fair. How had she not gone to Alaxia when she passed on? And Lysander, sweet, generous Lysander had always looked out for others. She inhaled a long breath, trying to remember those last days of her human life, but memories were still filtering in.

She gasped. "Sanura. Is she..."

"Ended by our ancestor. You'll meet her," Aesop said.

An angel landed beside them and wrapped an arm around Aesop's waist. He was tall and lean with a self-assured expression that made

4

Helena want to laugh, but the familiar way he embraced her brother had her eyes narrowing.

"Aesop. Who is this? A boyfriend? Are you old enough to date?"

The angel whose arm encircled Aesop possessively, snorted.

"Helena, I'm three thousand years old," Aesop said. "This isn't my boyfriend. He's my soulmate and we've been together in Alaxia for centuries. You were my older sister once, but my time has long surpassed yours. I am afraid you are the younger of us now."

"I'm Zadkiel," the angel said, holding out his free hand. "It's nice to meet you. I was overjoyed to learn Aniel's mate finally returned to him."

Helena stared at his outstretched hand, then up at his face. "Zadkiel... Do I... know you?"

He smiled. "We met once, briefly."

Aniel found her hand again, laced their fingers together, and tugged her to him. The desire to be close, to touch, was overwhelming and all her focus moved to the angel at her side. She inhaled his scent and sighed.

If anyone had asked her what the end of the world would look like, she never would have predicted it would be this.

"Wait. Where's Dina?"

CHAPTER 1

Peter

The ground rocked beneath his feet and shouts of dismay rose from the field of lavender as souls stumbled and fell. Peter scanned the distant horizon, searching for the cause of the disturbance, finding nothing but an expanse of purple swaying lazily on some imaginary breeze.

Yesterday, the boats had stopped arriving. Of the souls who remained in Sheol, there was a clear divide. Those who should have gone to Primoria were alert, anxious, and unsettled here. No amount of soothing earth magic funneled into the place seemed to put them at ease.

The other group listed aimlessly, swaying with the wind.

Until yesterday, some found their way to him every day, waking from some stupor, but when the boats stopped arriving, the souls slipped further into a state of catatonia.

The ground rumbled again, and Peter blinked. Was the line of trees encircling the field closer?

"Peter." He turned as Asher rushed to his side, small cheeks puffing in and out. "It's starting. The realms are colliding."

A cold weight settled in Peter's stomach.

The ground shuddered again, and this time he knew he wasn't imagining it. The trees were much closer. The field had shrunk by half.

He glanced back at the sphinx. "What does it mean for us?"

Asher pawed the earth. "We'll be on Earth soon."

"What about the souls who were meant for Primoria?"

Asher's eyes widened. "They were meant to freeze in the depths of Primoria. Now that it's gone, I fear they will meet some new and terrible end when we arrive on Earth."

When the ground rocked this time, half the field was gone in a blink, and half the souls with it. Peter swallowed, searching for Cassia among them. His mind conjured souls reforming on Earth, only to find themselves spiked on shards of ice or trapped beneath frozen lakes—bodies trapped beneath a mountain of snow.

He had to do something.

Dashing away from the sphinx, he stuffed his hand into his pocket, running a thumb over the crease marring the surface of the amulet he'd found lying on the ground moments before his death. He hadn't expected it to come with him to Sheol, but after so many years with it, it was a reassurance—a last comforting vestige of life on Earth.

Now he was returning to that place, but he wasn't sure what he would find there. Was Earth to be his new Hell? Would he arrive only to find himself trapped in some endless torture? Could he even die now that the world was ending?

His thumb rubbed a slow circle over the smooth gold as it warmed under his touch, catching on the groove of a crescent moon. He stopped after a short sprint on the banks of the river, mouth hanging open.

It had taken considerably less time than usual to arrive, but what shocked him most was the massive crack zigzagging along the bed of a bone-dry riverbed. Stretching into a distance that had always appeared hazy before, it now ended abruptly. Where the boats had disappeared into some distant horizon, unreachable to the likes of him, there was nothing. A black void.

"Peter."

His gaze darted left. "Cassia. Where are the others?"

"Some have already disappeared."

He nodded. "Get whoever's left, but don't waste time on those who don't want to come. We must leave now."

She dipped her chin, disappearing as quickly as she'd come.

Peter stepped into the dry riverbed, skirting the edge of the crack. He halted beside a cliff and glanced down. The ground rocked, and he nearly lost his footing, dancing back from the inky blackness. Leaning forward, he searched the nothingness for any sign of life. Darkness swallowed the light; where there might once have been a night sky, it was simply blank.

Closing his eyes, he listened. His hearing was still heightened, and far in the distance, he heard... running water. Could the river have sunk into some new realm?

Cassia appeared beside him and leaned forward. "You can't be serious."

He glanced back, spying the gathered mass of souls behind her. "Is this it?"

"More disappear by the minute."

He nodded. "What waits for us on Earth will be our reckoning. I'd rather take my chances with the void." He turned around, facing the crowd.

They pressed close to one another, glancing nervously at the blackness ahead, but many were darting looks over their shoulders at the shrinking mass of land behind them.

Peter lifted a hand. "I'm not asking any of you to come with me. But I'm not going to Earth to be dealt punishment for crimes I had no choice in committing. I'd rather face a permanent end than an eternity of torture. But you must each make up your own mind."

Grumbling responses followed and when the realm rattled underfoot the next time, the nothingness closed in.

"I'm going. Do what you must."

With that, he turned, leaping off the cliff's edge and desperately hoping he had made the right choice.

CHAPTER 2

Michael

Michael exhaled a long breath. It had been an age since he set foot on Earth. Memories of sweltering heat, baked clay, packed dirt and sweating bodies crowded together as they vied for space—drifted to the forefront of his mind. Reminders of the pungent smells they created chased them and he frowned.

He stared out the arched window of his room at spires of snow and ice. When his view overlooked the Heavens, it was easy to forget that time, but now, faced with the very real reminder of an age long gone, he feared the past could no longer be held at bay.

Pristine white feathers flapped, and he inhaled sharply as the broker of peace in his day landed lightly on his windowsill. He moved to stand beside it, holding out a hand. The creature eyed him warily but lifted on silent wings and landed on his outstretched hand.

"Come to convince me to join them?" he asked the bird, running fingers down its neck.

It cooed, warming a long-dead piece of his heart.

"They don't want me there. I would only dampen their mood."

The dove ducked its head before spreading both wings and launching out his window. He watched it go, sighing. Once, he would have led the charge to join the mortals in their revels and celebrate the victory.

Though it had been foretold, the end of the world had never been promised to the side of God. Some dark bit of his soul had been waiting to see how the cards would fall—fearing the worst and not daring to hope for anything good.

"Michael?"

Agony sliced through him. That voice made his chest constrict, as though the last dregs of air in the universe had been expelled from his lungs. He should turn and acknowledge her, but to look upon her was to taste the bitterness of all he'd endured. Jaw set, he stared out the window and prayed she would go. He inhaled a shallow breath, terrified to breathe in her scent. One whiff and he would fall at her feet; beg her to forgive his eternity of idiocy.

"We are going down. Would you..." Her pause was long enough that he thought she wouldn't ask, but when she spoke again, her voice was a caress against his ear, and he closed his eyes. "Come with us?"

Rows of blooming gardenia bushes filled his mind as warmth burned his back, The longing in his chest was enough to shatter him. Or it should have been—in a just world. In this world, he remained silent and motionless. When the pad of her finger brushed his bare shoulder, the worst kind of desire spiked through him.

"Please," he gasped, squeezing his lids tightly against the pain. "Please don't ask this of me."

Her touch evaporated, and slowly, minute by minute—an eternity later—her lingering scent faded.

When he opened his eyes, he was alone and could almost believe she'd never come.

CHAPTER 3

Peter

He was falling, but in the empty silence, he might have been floating. Memories he hadn't realized he'd lost drifted to the forefront of his mind and with them, a past that wasn't his own.

He was at the Graves estate, looking out the third-floor window on a cold, rainy night. Fat droplets hit the glass, splattering against the thin pane. As they streaked along its surface, stripes painted trails through the fog. Lightning cracked, and the world was lit for just long enough that the scene came into focus.

He pressed a hand to the window. "Claire!"

She couldn't hear him.

He raced from the room, down the stairs, and out the front door. "Claire!"

Flashes of blue light shot into the dark, and he skidded to a halt beside her.

"Get inside, Simon. I've got them," Claire panted. She threw up another ball of flame and hurled it at the hoard of inky shapes.

Wasting no time arguing with the stubborn girl, he lunged for the first demon, sinking his teeth into the side of its neck and draining it.

It slipped through his fingers, melting into blackness. White hot pain sliced along his arm and he gasped.

"Simon!"

Streaks of blue flame shot past his head, and two demons dissolved into nothing.

He screamed as fire erupted through his middle.

Claire shouted his name again. Rain-slicked arms wrapped around him as he sank to his knees, coldness tugging at his chest. He peered up at glimmering sapphire eyes glowing unnaturally bright on the moonless night.

"I'm sorry," he croaked.

"Shhhh," she whispered, running her free hand over his forehead. Her hands were frigid against his burning skin. "Don't talk."

He leaned into her. If he would finally die, at least it would be in the arms of the one he loved.

The scene changed, and he was tugged into a new memory.

"Will this save him?" The world was dark, but her voice was strong and sure.

"Yes, but we must also erase this night from his mind. He cannot know about our kind."

"Take them all."

"I'm sorry, Claire, if I heal the old wounds, his mind will struggle to reconcile itself against the truth. I can only take tonight's."

He struggled to open his eyes and witness this moment, but his lids were glued shut; no matter how he tried, they would not show him what he so desperately wanted to see. But in this strange, in-between state, he recognized that voice.

The orchestrator of so much of his life's pain and suffering.

Zophiel.

CHAPTER 4

Sophia

Sophia wiped her arm over her brow and straightened. As one of Sanura's creatures, she hadn't been able to sweat, but when the world was at its end, she had regained several of her human abilities—though she'd kept her speed and extra hearing.

"Sophia." Leah appeared beside her and she staggered back. She would never get used to how angels could simply appear and disappear at will.

"What is it, Sister?"

Leah wrapped her arms around her, not seeming to notice the state of her sweat-soaked shirt. "We have a problem." She glanced beyond the newly tilled land to the row of houses they'd begun occupying when they moved into this town. "Those houses won't be strong enough. We need something more defensive."

Sophia backed up, staring up at her slightly glowing friend. "Slow down. What happened?"

"Some souls in Sheol disappeared. Asher says they must be here, but no one can find them. It's not looking good and…" She bit her lip. "Simon—I mean' Peter is missing, too."

Sophia glanced back at the cookie-cutter houses with their flimsy doors and windows. There was no place high or low to hide from demons, but the souls bound for Primoria were something else. Were they human? Demon?

"I knew we'd have our work cut out for us, ending the last of the demons," Leah tucked her hair behind her ear. "But I hadn't considered the souls who never made it to Primoria."

"I need to warn the others." Sophia turned.

"Wait." Massive white wings appeared at Leah's back. "My party is needed to finish hunting the remaining demons. But Sophia, promise me you won't let them harm Peter if he shows up. I don't care who he's with, he wouldn't hurt any of you."

Sophia nodded and Leah's wings spread wide as she launched into the sky.

When she was gone, Sophia raced back to the home her coven was occupying. "Mother!"

Angeliki appeared in the doorframe. "What is it, Daughter?"

Sophia reached her, grabbing her hands. "There are missing souls that may be dangerous. We need to warn the others and prepare them to fight if it should come to that."

Angeliki nodded as General Vaughn stepped out behind her and wrapped an arm around her shoulders.

"General," Sophia said, dipping her chin.

He smiled in response, pressing a kiss to Angeliki's temple. "Everything alright?"

Sophia looked between her mother and the man who had become a permanent fixture in their lives in only a few short weeks. "Not really. We have another enemy to prepare for."

General Vaughn's mouth flattened into that thin line that meant he was readying himself to strategize. If anyone could see them through this next hurdle, it was the man who had escaped the destruction at the end of the world.

"Tell me."

She nodded and motioned for him to follow her inside.

CHAPTER 5

Peter

Peter's eyes flew open, his lips parting on a silent gasp. In this place, there was no air, no light, no gravity. There was nothing. He floated, or existed, or didn't. In the absence of everything, he wasn't sure what this was. Rebecca's face sifted through his mind and, like a gut punch, he was sucked into another memory.

"Simon, watch a movie with me?"

She was eighteen. He didn't have to guess. He remembered this one.

Claire laced her fingers through his and pulled him down the hall. They stopped outside the TV room. She glanced back, biting her lip, pink staining her cheeks. When Rebecca was on her deathbed for a second time, realizing baby Claire was actually her, she grabbed his hands, squeezing tightly and made him promise to look after her and any others that may come after.

"But," she'd wheezed, "you mustn't be with anyone but me. And only after I remember myself."

Who could refuse the dying wish of the one you loved?

Now, though, he saw how selfish that request had been, expecting him to spend his life alone while she was free to grow up loving anyone she chose. All while he could say or do nothing about it.

19

But the fear of a broken heart as he watched her grow to love another was misplaced. Claire had never been allowed to attend public school or to go anywhere, really. It was no wonder her first crush was one of the few people she knew. And so, he waited for the love of his life to return to him, hopeful and a little terrified.

"I've been waiting for this movie."

Peter followed her in, untangling their hands, and slid onto a chair beside the couch.

The lights went off and Claire moved to the television, twisting the knob, and bringing the screen to life. She adjusted the rabbit ears until the picture was crisp and sank back onto the couch, glancing over at him with her eyebrows bunched over her forehead. "It would be more comfortable on the couch."

Peter cleared his throat, staring at the screen. "I prefer a chair."

Loud music blared to life as title credits scrolled across the screen. They sat in silence as names of actors, the director, casting directors, and all the other people who had a hand in creating the film slid down the screen.

The words *Forever* panned onto the screen and abruptly disappeared. Some distant part of his mind reconciled the grainy footage and bad editing with what he knew of advancements in film before Claire flopped herself down on the couch huffing loudly.

He stared forward, gluing his eyes to the screen.

Claire ran her free hand through her hair, tugging her nails through curls, exhaling softly. Her breath, minty and clean, invaded his nostrils. She had brushed her teeth before the movie. Very unlike her.

On screen, someone was talking, but Peter tuned it out, listening to the beat of Claire's heart, steady and strong. Although Alexander had been draining her for years, she seemed healthy—a far cry from Rebecca's weakened state by this age.

She laughed and glanced at him. Their eyes met, light flashing across her face as the scene changed.

Her heart picked up speed, and the decadent scent of her desire filled the air.

Peter broke their stare first, turning back to the movie. He breathed shallowly, trying—and failing—not to be affected by her.

The soft *thump, thump, thump* of her heart picked up speed, and she leaned across the space between their chairs, palm landing on his thigh.

"I'll make popcorn," Peter said, jumping up.

He raced to the door and flipped the light switch. Not waiting for a response, he darted from the room and down the stairs to the kitchen. In the dark, he leaned against the counter, inhaling air free of her lingering scent.

He ran a hand down his pants, attempting to smooth down the arousal growing at just that one touch, and groaned. He would need to find reasons to be away from the estate. If he weren't careful, he would do something he'd regret and Rebecca would never forgive him for it.

Light footfalls on the third-floor landing roused him into motion and he moved to the pantry, pulling out a pan of stovetop popcorn. Lighting the wick to the stove, he set the pan down and faced it, shaking it slowly.

When hands came around his waist and Claire's warm body pressed against his back, he went rigid. Her cheek rested between his shoulder blades, as she exhaled a sigh.

Claire had never been so forward. Had she remembered? Was she back? Rebecca had not returned until Sarah was twenty-three, but was it possible she remembered sooner this time? If it wasn't Rebecca, it meant Claire was tired of waiting. She was making her move.

He was terrified to find out.

Instead, he remained frozen as her hands moved, sliding over the ridges in his abdomen up his chest. Popcorn began to sizzle and pop. Her hands moved south, finding the waistline of his pants and stopping. Not Rebecca.

"Claire."

Her hands froze, fingers flexing involuntarily. "Yeah?"

"What are you doing?"

Her arms vanished from around his waist.

He turned slowly.

Claire had backed up several inches. Fire blazed across her cheeks as she looked anywhere but at his face. "I thought..." She bit her lip, not meeting his gaze.

He stepped forward, tipping her chin up with a finger. "Hey. There's nothing to be embarrassed about, but. We can't—"

The red in her cheeks deepened, but her gaze lifted to him and embarrassment no longer clouded her eyes. "Why not? Is there someone else you love?"

Peter bit back a smile. Her fiery temper, even when they'd made no declarations to one another, warmed something inside him. "You are important to me."

Claire huffed out a disgruntled sigh. "I matter. Really?"

Peter did smile then. "You do. More than you could ever know." He turned, shaking the pan of popcorn.

Claire huffed loudly at his back. "So I matter, but not in that way."

Peter lifted the popcorn from the stovetop, twisting the burner off, and shook the pan a few times before moving away from Claire, and dumping its contents into a bowl. The smell of freshly popped corn and salt masked the scent of Claire's desire, but only slightly.

When he turned, she snatched the bowl from his hand, setting it on the counter. She stepped into his space, trapping him against the counter.

He backed up, hitting solid stone, and held up his hands. "Come on, Claire. You wanted to watch a movie."

Something playful glinted in her eye, and she leaned into him, pressing her body against his. His reaction was immediate and her eyes went wide as she felt his hard length growing against her stomach.

She pressed more firmly into him, lifting onto her tiptoes, eyes falling closed, and pressed her mouth to his.

Peter wrapped his fingers around Claire's shoulders, gently pushing her back and her eyes flew wide anger blazing to life. Hurt and rejection flashed across her face before she backed away, a tear sliding down her cheek.

"Claire, please. I'm sorry."

She swiped it from her cheek, and ran from the room.

He was frozen. He wanted to go to her, to comfort her, but it would only feed the desire that had been building between them for months. If he followed her now, she would give in to those feelings and when she remembered who she was, Rebecca would never forgive him.

The memory went dark. Peter was back in the ether, alone with his thoughts and emptiness. Some part of him wished he could have stayed in that memory a little longer. To do it over. If he could he would have followed. He would have held her and comforted her and told her how important she was to him.

He would have kissed her. What did it matter now anyway?

CHAPTER 6

Helena

Helena stopped beside a counter covered in shiny metal objects, each piece carved with such detail it must have taken the artisan months to create them. Surely these relics were recovered from some tomb or royal crypt; no mere peasant would have the fortune to commission such work.

She held up a rectangular object, examining it in the light. It buzzed, and she screamed, dropping it on the counter.

A deep laugh erupted beside her. She narrowed her eyes at Aesop. "What is so funny? The thing is possessed."

"I remember my first time seeing modern technology. It's called a phone, Helena."

"A what?"

"It was used to contact other people," Aesop continued. "When the realms converged, something knocked out all communication devices, so the army is trying to restore satellite capabilities."

"You're speaking in tongues, brother. What does any of that mean?"

Aniel appeared, pressing a kiss to Helena's forehead and lacing their fingers together. "Ah, I see you've found cell phones."

Helena tugged her hand free, backing up. "Will you both stop talking to me as though I know of what you speak?" She exhaled through her nose, working to calm her breathing. She'd been back a matter of weeks, and everyone treated her as if she should understand everything from this time and place.

It was hard enough attempting rudimentary conversation with the other humans who didn't speak her language. Learning her mother was gone, along with her other siblings and Dina... It had all been a great deal to process.

"Come on Hel. It's new to many people. If you spent more time among humans, you would adapt to our new world quicker." Aesop bumped her shoulder as he picked up a phone and held down a small rectangle along its edge. The glass surface refracting light lit up as if on fire, and shapes began appearing and disappearing across its face.

Helena stumbled backward. "What sort of magic is that?"

Aesop tossed the object to a soldier sitting in a chair made entirely of metal and he caught it, fingers moved rapidly. A person appeared trapped behind the glass.

Helena gasped, pressing a finger to the smooth surface. "Is it a spell?" She whispered.

"Come, my dove," Aniel said, holding out his hand. "Let me show you the world you live in."

Helena cast a nervous glance over her shoulder at her brother. He was so much like Lysander, it hurt. But there were traces of their mother in him, too.

She wrapped her fingers around Aniel's, letting out an involuntary sigh when their souls connected. He scooped her up in his arms, and her chest hummed with the rightness of their bodies pressed together. Visions of the past several nights—their skin hot against each other, slick from lovemaking, and Aniel's fingers tangled in her hair—flashed through her mind.

He lifted off the ground, rising into the air, and soon they were high above the camp and its dwellings. From this height, she saw it was a loose circle, surrounded on three sides by spiked peaks. Atop the highest mountains, a gleaming castle rested.

The rainbow bridge she'd traveled glittered in the midday sun, carving a multihued path through their new village.

There were several of these camps around Colorado, but she and those bound to the angels had remained here, beside the castle. She and Aniel had spent their nights in his room, and guilt twisted in her gut at the thought of so many making do with what they had on Earth while she languished in the finest down bed she'd ever experienced.

Aniel's nose brushed against her neck. "Would you like to see Athens?"

Helena leaned into his warmth. "Show me your favorite place."

Aniel's breathing hitched against her side and was shallow for several seconds. When he spoke, his voice was a low and rough. "You were the only place that mattered. The world held no joy without you in it."

Helena's heart thrummed in her chest, her skin heating, and she smiled. "Very well. Show me everything I've missed."

CHAPTER 7

Peter

Peter knew now what this was. Though they weren't going in order, he was lost to his regrets. He wasn't even sure there was a pattern to them. They came upon him, forced him to relive everything he wished he could do differently, and made him watch as he destroyed the lives of everyone around him.

Peter was in Hell.

Rachel skipped into his room like she owned it. She always had. Robert hung back, hovering in the doorway.

"Good evening, Rachel."

She smiled that impish grin and spun in a circle, pleased with herself about something. He wouldn't have to wait long to find out; like all the others, Rachel had no patience. Her gaze darted back to Robert, and she motioned him into the room.

Wide blue eyes fell on Peter, stretched out atop the bed, a book splayed across his lap, then back to Rachel. He shook his head. Robert rarely spoke, and when he did, he was a quiet, grave thing, full of contemplation and foreboding.

"Get in here," Rachel demanded.

Robert's brows furrowed as his head shook back and forth again, and Rachel rolled her eyes at her brother.

It had been fascinating to watch the two of them grow. Truly, Rebecca's qualities were divided between the pair. All of her quiet introspection lived with Robert, while all her hot-headed tempestuousness lived with Rachel.

Rachel danced forward and sat at the end of Peter's bed. "We found something."

Reaching for his bookmark, Peter slid it into his book and closed it. "What did you find?"

"A secret room."

Peter's stomach flipped. "Where?"

"On the fifth floor."

His reaction was both relief and intrigue. At eleven, the twins were nearly the same age Claire had been when Alexander began draining her life. He lived in near terror of the day they would be called down to his underground workshop to take from them, too.

In the distant part of his mind that knew he wasn't truly living *this* moment, he wondered why he couldn't remember there being a fifth floor in the mansion.

"Come on." Without waiting to see if he would follow, Rachel hopped up and skipped out of the room, dragging her brother along.

Peter stood, following the pair as they moved, twin raven-haired heads bobbing down the hall. He smiled to himself.

Rachel had always been odd. At eight, when she had proclaimed she and Robert would forever wear their hair the same, he should have known she meant it. At eleven, they still sported the same cut. It was too long for a boy and too short for a girl, but no one ever told them so and every trip to the barber resulted in the same matching cut.

They turned right at the end of the hall, where Rachel boldly shoved the door to her father's room open.

Peter froze outside in the doorframe. Petrified to the spot. "Rachel," he hissed.

"Come on!"

After a moment's hesitation, he followed, moving on light feet, fully prepared to drag them away at speed if Alexander was somewhere inside.

He wasn't. When Rachel crossed the room to the old bookcase that had once belonged to Pearl and tipped several of the books back at once, a click sounded. The bookshelf popped open, revealing a narrow, winding set of stairs.

"Robert." On cue, Robert produced a lighter from his pocket and handed it to Rachel. She lifted it to an old wall sconce, covered in dust and cobwebs, and lit it. Up they went. Peter followed, more curious by the second.

Why didn't he remember any of this?

At the top of the stairs, Rachel flicked the lighter again at the wick of another wall sconce. It flared to life, faintly illuminating a long hallway. Peter stepped around the twins, twisting the candle off its sconce, and moved down the hall, lighting the rest as he went.

When the narrow passage was lit well enough to see, he returned the first to its place and held out his hands. The twins grasped his fingers in their clammy palms, hugging tightly to his sides. Feet kicked up years of caked dust as they shuffled forward, stopping outside a single door.

There were no windows, no external light shone through any cracks or crevices, and the oppressive weight of a silencing spell draped itself over every surface. His gut churned. Whatever they found on the other side of this door, there would be no going back from it. But even if he'd wanted to turn around, he was a passenger in a memory lost to him and could only watch as he released Robert's hand and twisted the knob.

The door creaked loudly. Peter stepped through as a gust of wind sucked the air inside. Something in the room's corner inhaled sharply.

Shoving the children behind him, he lifted his hands, prepared to fight.

A creak sounded, and his vision adjusted to the darkness. The figure in the corner was hardly more than bones, but its chest rose, taking in a rattling breath. Long strands of white hair fell down its back, dragging on the floor.

He glanced back. Rachel's bright blue eyes were lit with delighted curiosity. Robert seemed to have disappeared into his own mind, as he did sometimes.

"If I tell you to run. Do it."

Rachel's gaze darted to Peter, and she scowled. "I'm not scared."

The thing in the corner inhaled another rattling breath, bones shuffling in an old wooden chair.

Peter crept closer and Rachel stubbornly dug her nails into his hand when he tried to shake her loose. He sighed, taking her with him as he drew nearer.

Peter halted, frozen in place as bones turned eyeless sockets toward them. A long sighing exhale escaped its lipless mouth, and Peter took a shaky breath of his own.

Steeling himself, he took another step forward.

The figure wore a dress reminiscent of the nineteen twenties, possibly earlier. Its bony feet were clad in low heels, ankles crossed over each other as if it were a lady, sitting for tea.

"Who are you?" he whispered.

Its head tilted as if it could see him, but unnaturally quickly, the skeletal head's sockets darted past him to the door.

Peter spun around and pulled Rachel against him.

Outlined in the flickering light, the imposing frame of Alexander Graves filled the doorway.

"I see you've found Pearl."

CHAPTER 8

Michael

Michael crunched loudly over gravel as he stepped down onto Earth. The feeling was all at once new and reminiscent of a past he'd buried and tried to forget.

Around him, creatures busied themselves with their afterlife. Humans, sphinxes and angels worked side by side to rebuild what was destroyed.

It was a new world, one where humans no longer feared the creatures they dwelt beside, and demons no longer hid in the shadows. Some heavy weight, long carried, lifted a fraction. Could he give leave to believe for even a moment that a future existed without pain, suffering and death?

A human child raced past him, kicking rocks behind him as he went. Children—humanity's hope and innocence. Michael had forgotten about them. How had the memory of such perfect creatures been buried so far in the recesses of his memory?

Someone laughed, and he glanced toward the sound. Laughter. What a thing it had once been. It held the power to soothe the soul and mend any ache. *Her* laugh erupted in his mind, and he staggered as though he'd been struck. A memory. Not real. He hadn't heard her laugh in a thousand years. More.

The laugh sounded again, and his gaze moved to the creature resting against a tree. Humans and creatures alike surrounded her, and she tipped her head back, letting out another loud guffaw.

His feet moved, drawing him toward the group before he knew where he was going. Michael reached the edge of their circle, standing several feet away. One woman looked up, eyeing him warily. He tucked his wing behind his back, straightening his shoulders. She looked away, and he turned.

"Hey."

His gaze moved back to the creature who had been laughing in the group's center, and he raised an eyebrow.

"I haven't seen you before. What's your name?"

Michael's lips fell into a flat line. "You would recognize one as disfigured as I. Suffice to say, I am a stranger to you."

A grin split her face. "Well, Stranger, I'm Vassi. Nice to meet you."

The corner of his mouth lifted, but he smothered the emotion creeping in. "I'd prefer you not address me at all, human."

Vassi's smile fell, some of her effortless joy winking out.

Bitter anger washed over him. He'd done that. He'd taken some of her happiness—and for what? Because he was in pain. Because he suffered. It was selfish. And it was why he had left the humans to revel after he'd given so much of himself to save them all those centuries ago.

He turned away, striding along the outskirts of their makeshift village, scanning it for any sign of Raphael.

Or *her*.

As he rimmed the encampment, his step lightened. Although this place was frigid, and it was clear rations were low, none fought. No tempers rose. There was a calm among them he'd never seen; so many humans packed together, working in concert with one another to achieve their goals.

Somehow, without the influence of his fallen brother or the demons he had created, these creatures lived harmoniously.

When he last set foot on the mortal plane, the Earth ran red with their hate and bigotry. He hardly dared imagine a future where humans co-existed without a drop of blood spilled. Yet as he continued, some long-buried emotion resurfaced.

Hope.

CHAPTER 9

Peter

"Simon. Take Rachel and Robert to my room and wait for me. I'll meet you there."

Peter strained uselessly against Alexander's command as he pulled Rachel with him, stopping outside the door to the strange hidden room and wrapping his hand around Robert's shoulder, dragging him away.

Rachel didn't fight, too aware of his inability to refute the orders. Robert was blank-eyed as he marched ahead; Peter cursed his stupidity for not discouraging this adventure. They would certainly be punished.

In Alexander's underground lair, he released them both, spinning to face Rachel. "Go. Run before he gets here. I can't leave, but you can."

Rachel crossed her arms over her chest. "I'm not leaving you."

"Please, you don't know what he's capable of. Take Robert and go."

That hollow queasy feeling was back in Peter's stomach. There was a reason he'd never known when Alexander's experiments began on the twins. He'd always thought it happened when he was away from the estate. Now he feared it was because the memory had been stolen from him.

Why, though? Alexander didn't care. Wouldn't have taken the time to remove a memory that would only cause him pain later. He was missing something.

Rachel's eyes narrowed, and she planted her feet in the dirt. "I'm not going anywhere. If Father wants to hurt us, he will. And if we aren't here when he comes down, he'll only punish you for it."

Even now, Rebecca's stubborn, brave streak was evident in Rachel. Terror sliced down Peter's spine. Alexander enjoyed breaking things, and Rachel had too much strength for her own good. Robert and Rachel had been spared the worst of Alexander's machinations thus far, but a countdown clock had begun ticking—it was only a matter of time before the worst happened.

Heavy footfall reverberated in the winding stair, sounding his approach.

"Get back."

Some of Rachel's bravado fell away when she heard Alexander's footsteps; she ducked behind Peter, tugging Robert with her.

The door swung wide, and Alexander stepped in. He surveyed the room coolly, his gaze landing on Rachel. He smiled.

"I think it's time you know the truth, girl."

Rachel's squeaky reply was cut off when a ball of orange flame burst to life in Alexander's palm.

Peter moved to block Alexander's path. "Don't touch them."

Ignoring him, Alexander sent the ball of flame into the air, and tugged his worn leather journal from his pocket, moving to the center of the room and setting it on the table. "Rachel, come."

Under no compulsion, she remained where she was.

Alexander looked up, frowning. "Come or your brother dies. I don't need both of you."

Her eyes went round, glancing back at Robert standing in the corner, and then to Alexander. She stepped around Peter. He moved to block her, but she scowled up at him. He fisted his hands at his sides, letting her pass. When she reached Alexander, he pointed to a place on the floor beside him and she moved to stand there.

"Do you know what a necromancer is?"

Rachel shook her head, suddenly looking very young.

"It's a type of witch. A very powerful type of witch, responsible for bringing a person back from the dead."

Peter slowly inched toward Robert, blocking him from view.

"You—abomination that you are—were born from such a creature," Alexander continued. "The creature made by a necromancer." He licked the tip of his finger, turning pages in his journal. "Ah. Here we are."

His sharp gaze landed on Rachel. "How old are you now? Nine, ten?"

"I'm eleven," Rachel said, jutting out her chin.

"Very good."

Peter knew, in the core of his very being, what came next. Unless he stopped it. "I haven't fetched you a new demon in days, Alexander. Let me bring you one."

Alexander looked up. "No need. I have a perfectly good source right here." He waved a dismissive hand at him, then pointed his finger at the page in his book he'd been about to read from.

"Please. Alexander, give her a few more years."

"What difference does it make? They all die in the end."

Rachel's lip quivered, but tears never came. "Did you kill my mother?"

"Enough questions. Get on the table."

A single tear slipped down Rachel's cheek as she backed up. "No. Tell me what you did to my mother."

Alexander let out an exasperated sigh, gaze darting to Peter. "Simon. Put her on the table."

Rachel backed up, turning to run. Peter was faster catching her around the waist. "I'm so sorry," he whispered into her hair.

Rachel wriggled in his grasp as he carried her back to the table and set her atop it. The moment he released her, she hopped down, bolting for the door.

"I'm losing patience. Simon, bring her back and hold her down."

Peter fought the compulsion, but it was no use. Rachel made a valiant effort, reaching the third step before he caught her.

"Please Alexander, don't do this. I can bring you as many demons as you wish. A dozen, one hundred."

Alexander snorted, coming to stand over Rachel as she squirmed under Peter's hold.

He tried to loosen his grip, to keep his fingers from digging into her shoulders, but the harder she fought, the tighter his grip became, compelled by the magic to keep her there. There would be bruises. He exhaled a shaky breath. "Use Robert. His essence is stronger. I can sense it."

Horror rose in Peter. He wanted to take the words back, to swallow them whole, but there was no changing the past.

Alexander's eyebrow rose as he looked up at the boy who hadn't moved from his place by the wall. "It can't be."

Peter lifted a shoulder. "I don't pretend to know how essence works, but his calls to me in a way hers never has. Perhaps she got all the temper, and he got all the soul." His heart sank, and he wondered if he'd found a way to bury this memory so he wouldn't have to live with the shame of his actions.

"I hate you. I hate you!" Rachel screamed. Her narrowed eyes burned into him, then turned pleading as she looked to Alexander. "He's lying! My brother's half a person. Don't hurt him. Whatever it is, he won't survive it. Use me!"

"Simon, put her in the shackles and bring me the boy."

"Run. Robert, run!" Rachel thrashed like a wild beast as she bucked in Peter's arms. She kicked him in the stomach and he grunted, not meeting her eyes. She would never forgive him. The feeling was mutual.

Every moment of this agony burned in his chest. Like the others, he too, was a victim of Alexander's cruelty, but in this moment, he had chosen wrong and there was no undoing it.

The memory evaporated, and he was floating again, drifting in a place with no sight, sound, or smell. Given all he now knew, he wondered if he truly would have made a different choice. After he'd seen what would become of them, how easy it was to say he would have done it differently.

CHAPTER 10

Sophia

S ophia stretched out on her makeshift bed and stared up at the roof of her stolen home. Some part of her despised this new life, living in homes that once belonged to humans who were not coming back.

Those who had died and gone to Alaxia before the war were restored, but so far, it appeared any who died after the realms converged were not. Worse, some of those in Sheol had assimilated, but the souls who would have been bound for Primoria were still missing. Sophia was no longer confident they would return. It would break Leah's heart if Peter was truly gone, but Sophia feared it was much worse than that. It likely meant he did not want to be found.

"Sophia." Vassi's whispered voice called through her window and she sat up. "You better come see."

Sophia slid out of bed and raced after Vassi, following her to the center of their new town. They'd converted an old Dollar General into the town's meeting space and it looked like half the community had shown up for whatever was happening. In the group's center, General Vaughn—flanked by two of his men—was holding one of Sophia's sisters. One she'd lost all hope of ever seeing again.

"Cassia," she breathed.

Several people talked loudly over one another, shouting to be heard. Cassia's sharp gaze darted to her, and she scowled.

"Everyone, please," the general said, and the room quieted. "We found this creature attempting to steal from our food stores. I don't want to enforce rank here, but as we've yet to establish any form of government, I must insist we have rules that protect us."

Several people spoke again, some translating for each other, and heads nodded.

"I'm not suggesting anything rash, but stealing food puts everyone at risk."

More whispered ascent.

"I propose we lock her up until we can hold a trial to determine her punishment."

Sophia stepped forward, prepared to speak up, but her mother appeared in the crowd and lifted both hands. "We deal with our own," she proclaimed in Greek. The general's brow furrowed in confusion, and she repeated herself in English.

"Angelica, I understand she may have been in your coven once, but the others told me she did not come back to fight with your daughter. She was forced to stay behind." He gave her a meaningful look.

Sophia crossed the room to stand beside her mother. "You only hold her because she allows it. She's too fast or strong for your kind to keep her locked up."

"Hang her!" someone shouted.

Sophia's stomach flipped at the violent outburst, and she searched the crowd for the owner of the voice. "We do not kill one another. The time for vile deeds has passed." She glared around the room at the humans who relied on her and her sisters to patrol their town for demons, daring them to contradict her.

As she met their eyes, they looked away, pink coloring their cheeks. She returned her focus to the general. "I will speak with my sister."

His brows furrowed, but he nodded. "My men will go with you."

She dipped her chin, and one of the soldiers shoved Cassia forward. Sophia ushered them out the door, following, and the crowd dispersed.

In her home, Sophia threw her arms around her sister. Cassia stiffened in her embrace, hands still secured behind her back. "Why did you let them bind you?" Sophia whispered low enough that only another creature would hear her.

"I wanted to see what they would do."

Sophia stepped back, looking her cousin over for injuries. "What happened to you? Where are the others?"

"We're here. Most of us. And we've been starving. Outside your little towns, there isn't much left of the world. They look to me for aid and I have nothing to offer them. I'd hoped if I came, your community would help us. I see now they won't."

Sophia pursed her lips. "You didn't *ask*, Cassia, you stole. We are struggling just like the rest and we've had to work hard for what we have."

Cassia ripped her arms free of their restraints. "It was a mistake to come here. Let me go and we'll leave you in peace."

"Join us, Cassia. Work for your food and you will eat. More hands mean more crops. We aren't saying no, simply that you cannot steal what you did not help grow."

Cassia frowned, glancing over her shoulder at the men guarding the door. "We're ten times stronger than them and we can bend elements to our will. Why are you doing all the work for them? Together, we could live well."

Sophia backed up, twirling a strand of hair around her finger. "Cassia, your sisters are here. Would you leave them to starve? To be killed by rogue demons still roaming the land?"

"They left me to fend for myself when Elizabeth came. I was the only one with fire magic in our coven, and Elizabeth and her creatures tortured me for days. None of our sisters tried to help me when I lay freezing and dying in a cell. Now you ask me to aid them?"

A tear formed on Sophia's lashes. "What happened to you, cousin? You loved your sisters once."

"That was before I died. Before Sanura gave me a second chance."

"Sanura?" Sophia gasped, backing up. "What do you mean?"

Cassia's mouth twisted into a cruel smile. "Did you think you were the only one she spoke to in Sheol? She found me first and offered to help me in exchange for a small favor."

Sophia shook her head. "Sister, what did you do?"

Cassia closed the space between them, reaching under her shirt. Her fingers ran along a gold chain Sophia hadn't noticed and tugged a slender locket out.

She moved, wrapping her fingers around Sophia's throat too quickly for her to stop it, exhaling hot breath over her mouth. "All I had to do was get this from Simon's pocket and bring it here. The rest would be revealed when the time was right." Cassia's grip tightened around Sophia's neck. She gasped and dug her nails into Cassia's hand, tugging uselessly.

"Pythia?" Vassi asked from the doorway.

Sophia tried to call out to warn her, but only a wheezing gasp left her lips as Vassi stepped into the room. Cassia whipped her sharp nails out, slicing across her friend's neck and chest, sending her staggering backward. A hand flew to her throat as Vassi let out a gurgled scream.

Shouts rang out and the soldiers on the other side of the door rushed in with weapons raised. Outside, boots thundered over the ground as they raced toward them.

Sophia tried to wave them off, to stop them from shooting at her sister, but her lungs screamed for air as spots dotted her vision.

The pressure around her throat slackened, and she dropped to her knees. Cassia backed up and darted through the window beside her.

A crack sounded as metal whizzed overhead, but Cassia was already gone.

People flooded in, speaking animatedly, calling out to one another for answers.

Vassi slumped against the wall, and Sophia crawled on hands and knees toward her. In this new state, they bled once more—they could *die*. She pressed down hard on the wounds, feeling slick warmth under her palms.

"Breathe, Vassi. It's okay. I'll find a healer. Leah... Leah!"

Thick crimson oozed between Sophia's fingers and a tear leaked down her cheek as Vassi's eyes went wide with terror. Her inhales were labored, her lips white as she sucked desperately for air.

Loud protests behind Sophia had her glancing back as an angel with a single wing shoved his way into the room, knocking people aside, before kneeling beside them.

"Move Nasdaqu-ush," he commanded.

Sophia sat up, releasing Vassi's bloody neck.

A lock of golden hair fell across his tanned face, marring Sophia's view of his strong jawline. He looked so like Raphael, but a hardness in his eyes spoke of grief beyond anything even Sophia could imagine. She had never seen an angel who only possessed a single wing.

He cupped his palms over the wound and a soft white light spilled through the seams in his fingers. "Look at me, Vassi. Open your eyes."

His gaze was intent on her sister, and Sophia watched him work, wondering when the two had met.

Vassi blinked, eyes coming into focus as she stared up at the angel, a a smile tugging at the corners of her mouth. "You came back." The words were cracked and rasping.

He grumbled something in a low voice, but his mouth twitched. When he lifted his hands, faint white lines zig-zagged down her neck and across her chest. Slowly, the color was returning to her cheeks and lips.

"Thank you, Stranger." she breathed.

Sophia's brows furrowed at the bridge of her nose. *Stranger?*

The angel leaned back, giving Vassi room to sit up before holding a hand out. She took it, climbing to her feet, and Sophia's gaze darted between the pair as they stared at one another, oblivious to their audience.

"Call me Michael."

CHAPTER 11

Peter

Peter lifted the newspaper, sipping tea as he read through the paper. Valentina stopped beside him, pressing her lips to his temple. "Good morning, my love."

He smiled up at her. "Dinner at Gallagher's?"

"I'd like that." Her thick mane of shining hair whipped around as she spun, scooping up her purse and letting herself out. In the doorway, she blew him a kiss.

His gaze fell to the obituaries section, and he continued scanning. It wasn't the most practical way to search for new clients—certainly not his only avenue, either. But back when he'd started this practice, it had been much more common to find business this way and somehow the habit had stuck.

Alexandra Graves

May 6, 2000 - September 9, 2017

The sole remaining member of the Graves line and a beautiful soul, Allie Graves, born to Rachel and Robert Graves, left this world unexpectedly on Thursday night. A passion for...

Peter stumbled backward, toppling his chair as he tripped over it, backing away from the article.

This wasn't one of Peter's forgotten memories, but it hurt no less the second time. It had been twelve years since Alexander finally succumbed, his body no longer able to survive even with essence feeding him. Twelve years where he had carved out a life.

After four years of searching for Rachel and Robert at Alexander's command, he knew they were safe and so was baby Allie. Some invisible cord pulled taut all these years, had finally loosened.

His mind—detached from this moment in history—knew what that feeling was: the binding Zophiel had placed upon him.

His phone rang, and he held it up. Valentina's name flashed across the screen. He stared at it, trying to make sense of the words, when everything inside him screamed to run to the nearest roof and fling himself off.

Peter had failed her; he had dared carve a piece of happiness from an otherwise drab existence for himself and it had cost Rebecca her life. He'd felt it. Felt it and thought he was having a heart attack. He should have known. But it was too soon... She was only seventeen.

Why had he been so selfish these twelve years? He stared around the starkly white high-rise apartment he'd purchased when he moved into the city, intent on making a life for himself.

A life. What a joke. At his core, he hadn't been alive in nearly a century. Who did he think he was, making a mockery of that? Thoughts swirled in his mind as though he were having them now instead of in this past version of himself.

All the guilt—all the regret—hit him hard. Then a new thought filtered in, one that belonged to Peter. *Gabriel.* Gabriel had been the one to bring her back from the dead. If Simon had been there, if he'd protected her, Gabriel would never have interfered.

She would have lived to twenty-five, had a child, and started all over again, but this time, Alexander would have been gone. He could have had that life with Allie; though it was a hard life, a lonely one, it was better than this.

His phone rang again in the memory, and he answered. "Hello?"

"Are you okay? I called, and you didn't answer."

"I'm fine." His voice was robotic, his mind a cyclone of bitter retorts.

"Gallaghers doesn't have availability tonight. Do you want to go to La Grande?"

"Sure."

"Simon..." When he didn't reply, Valentina swallowed audibly. "I love you."

"You too." He hung up, slipping the phone in his pocket.

Peter swiped his wallet and keys from the dining table, and left his apartment and his New York life.

Blackness swallowed the memory, hurtling him forward in time.

On a dark street, well after midnight, a tall, lithe form crept among the shadows. A sword nearly the length of her arm was strapped to her back, and she kept her head down. She seemed invisible in the crowd, but he was no stranger to humans ignoring what they did not want to see.

Abruptly, she turned a corner.

He darted after and pressed against a wall, ducking behind a trash bin as she drew her sword and sliced it through a demon. Pride swelled in his chest.

It had taken him almost six years to find her after the night he'd read her obituary.

In that time, he had prepared for her return, setting up her estate to be returned to her care after it had nearly been seized for non-payment of taxes, restoring electricity, working tirelessly to un-list the property from every real estate site he found it on while driving away potential buyers.

After scrubbing her death record, he filed all the paperwork to ensure Alexander's remaining funds would go to her and diverted a portion of his firm's income to her trust.

Now there was nothing left but to set her on the path back to her home. Where she would remember everything.

Something was different this time, though. There was no child. What could it mean? His current self knew, but his former self hadn't come to any logical conclusions yet. One thing was certain, without a child, this was her last life. Whether she lived to ninety or twenty-five like all the other times, he wanted to make the most of it.

If it was their only chance at a life without Alexander, he would take whatever they got and end his own miserable existence the day she took her last breath.

CHAPTER 12

Helena

Aniel swooped low over a sparkling blue ocean, a spray of sea foam splashing Helena's cheeks. She stretched tentative fingers towards the frigid water; Aniel dipped lower, giving her better access. She couldn't have imagined how large Earth was back when Greece seemed like the whole world and Athens its center.

"My city is buried beneath these waves?"

Yes, my dove, Aniel said into her mind. *We're just above the Acropolis.*

Warmth buzzed in Helena's chest when the words filled her mind, a gentle caress against her soul, and she smiled, glancing back at her perfect mate.

Below them, a dark shape swam under the water, matching their speed, and she yanked her hand back, as a beast of a creature broke the surface. A massive serpent's head rose, blocking their path. Helena swallowed her scream as Aniel halted midair, hovering just out of snapping distance of the great scaled monster.

Keen eyes observed them as a long tongue darted from its mouth, tasting the air. Helena cringed back, pressing herself tightly against her mate's chest. *Aniel, fly! It will eat us!*

She won't harm us, Dove. Aniel's arms tightened around her, calming some of her terror. He spoke aloud, the words foreign to Helena, and the sea serpent hissed a reply in the same strange language.

What does she say?

Sheol has dissolved, and the humans trapped there have fallen to Earth, he said into her mind. *We must warn the others.*

The serpent spoke again, and Aniel dipped his chin before launching into the sky. A thrill of excitement shot through Helena as they soared. When her feet first left the ground, her stomach had dropped like a stone, but she'd opened her eyes and felt nothing but wonder as her wide world shrank away. Soaring over the peaks of majestic mountains and across stretches of endless blue, she was free for the first time in her existence.

Peering down at the shrinking creature, she gasped when it leaped from the ocean, spiraling into the air before dipping and shooting beneath deep cerulean waves. Its dark shadow shot away, quicker even than Aniel had flown, and Helena watched in wonder as it disappeared along a never-ending horizon of blue.

What was that beast and where has it gone?

She's called Leviathan. She goes to her mate, returned to her after so many centuries apart.

Another serpent such as she?

No, my dove. Her mate is Behemoth, a land-dwelling beast.

Aniel dipped left. In the distance, Helena spied the peaks of familiar mountains.

But how can two be together when one lives on land and the other in the sea?

Aniel was silent for a long moment and a great sorrow filled her as his emotions swelled inside her.

They cannot.

A dark speck raced toward them, and Helena squinted to make out the angel who approached. Zadkiel's features came into focus as he swung around to fly beside Aniel. "Brother," he said. "There is unrest among the humans in Colorado."

"What has happened?"

"The souls bound for Primoria have returned to Earth. They have stolen crops, and a Nasdaqu-ush was injured. The humans are calling for blood."

Helena's heart beat unsteadily. Would they kill them? What would happen to those who died now when Heaven and Hell no longer existed?

Rest easy, Dove. The humans will see reason. They are upset now, but they will calm down. Aniel's emotions were clouded with doubt, but she couldn't tell if it was because he didn't believe his own words or something else worried him.

They raced over pock-marked, scorched land covered in debris and the remnants of humanity's last stand. Helena had not been present for it, but what remained told a story of death and destruction. She would not have wished to be among the humans in those final days, and her heart ached for them.

They touched down at the center of the makeshift village near the castle. The bright multihued rainbow path all had traveled to leave Aniel's fields was gone, making it impossible for any to enter the castle's high perch atop the mountain without wings or a winged escort.

Leah and her mate Gabriel lived among the seraphim who remained with the humans, but many others had returned to their old rooms, finding comfort in the familiar when they were not hunting down the remaining demons hiding on Earth.

The door to one of the human homes swung wide and Aesop stepped out, shielding his eyes from the bright midday sun. A grin split his face when he spied his mate and he wiped his hands on his oddly clothed legs. Jeans, he'd called the material. They looked terribly uncomfortable, and Helena was not yet prepared to give up her silks and robes for the clothing modern humans wore.

"You found them," Aesop said, wrapping an arm around Zadkiel's waist.

"They were nearly here when I spied them."

Aniel set Helena down, stepping forward to clasp forearms with Aesop. A twinge of jealousy stoked a fire in Helena's blood as it reminded her that these three had been companions for centuries while she was trapped in Aniel's throat. How different might it all be now if she'd been free to accept him as her mate long ago? How comfortable she might have been in jeans, moving among people.

Blowing out a breath, she trailed the trio as they moved through the village, Aesop speaking animatedly of the events that had transpired while they were away. A Nasdaqu-ush had attacked their stores, and Vassi was injured. Michael had saved her.

Aniel's shock at hearing this news had Helena scrunching her nose. She had never met Michael or Vassi. She scolded herself for not taking more time to get to know the people she would spend the rest of eternity with, resolving to seek them out.

Aniel paused, holding out a hand. *Perhaps avoid Michael, Dove.*

She took it, warmth bleeding through her at his touch. *Why?*

His lips twitched, but his brows furrowed, and a deep V formed between them. *He was dealt a blow many centuries ago. One he could never recover from. I fear for your safety should his anger be stoked.*

"We're forming scouting parties," Aesop continued. "Seraphim are scouring the terrain. Your aid would be appreciated."

"What about me? What can I do?" Helena straightened, staring up at her brother.

"Remain in camp, sister. Assist the humans with their harvest. They have no love for those living in the castle who do not take part in the labor. You do yourself no favors by separating yourself from them."

Helena's cheeks warmed. She hadn't asked where the food came from—hadn't thought to. In her time, it was provided, and she gave little thought as to how.

Aniel squeezed her hand, glancing at her before returning his gaze to her brother. "I am to blame. It has been so long. I wanted her to myself for a while."

Aesop smiled and clapped her mate on the back. "Of course, of course! But now that you'll join your brothers, Helena will have nothing but time on her hands to lend a hand." He winked at her. "Time to get your nails dirty, Sister."

Helena scowled at her brother as the memory of that very speech flashed in her mind. "That was thousands of years ago. You cannot still be upset with me." She tugged her hand from Aniel's, crossing her arms over her chest.

The group stopped outside a home made of the same strange material as all the others in this village, but it was painted blue with a bright red door. The color reminded her of blood, and she grimaced. What an odd color for a door.

It swung wide and Sophia, the witch who was faster than anyone else in camp, stepped out. Helena felt the unnatural tug of magic at her core and was involuntarily pulled toward her.

Sophia smirked. "Helena, right?"

Her accent was so familiar, yet entirely different. She'd spoken the words in Greek, but they were hard to understand, nonetheless.

"Yes," Helena said. "I've heard you are called Pythia."

Sophia nodded. "Though I'm not your coven's seer, you may call me Pythia if you like."

Helena stiffened. "Indeed, a member of my coven requires a special set of skills you do not possess."

Sophia's eyes twinkled, and she held up a hand. The ground rocked beneath them and Helena stumbled before catching herself. It shook again, and dirt and debris flew up as a geyser burst from the earth, whipping madly around the witch.

It drenched Helena, and she backed up, mouth falling slack. The others in their group seemed unsurprised by this show of power, Aesop grinning openly. Sophia stepped forward and Helena took an involuntary step back.

"I may not possess all four elemental gifts," she continued, "but the ones I command, I do so with a strength you never shall."

CHAPTER 13

Peter

Rebecca's eyes narrowed, and Peter backed up, holding out a hand. "Rebecca please. I'm trying to save you."

No, he pleaded. *Please, not this memory.* He remembered this one. Why did he have to relive it?

Tears welled along her lashes and streamed down her face. "Why did you go?" Her voice cracked as she shouted the question at him.

"I... I was trying to find a way to break the curse."

Rebecca backed up as her fingers ignited in bright blue flame.

Peter held up a hand, attempting a placating gesture, but the fire that had begun at her fingertips raced up her arms, cresting the top of her head down her legs. In moments, the room lit in a blinding sapphire hue, and Peter was hurtled backward.

He landed hard against the wall and his vision dimmed momentarily before bright white seared his retinas. This was new.

Broad wings, nearly dipped in silver, hovered a moment before landing beside him. His gaze solidified on Zophiel's face.

"What are you doing here?" Peter choked on the last word, shocked he could speak in a memory.

Zophiel's iridescent fingers touched his forehead. Somehow more brilliant than they had been in life.

"Now that I'm gone, my spells are unwinding. "

He nodded, knowing those words were for present him and not the Simon who'd lived this moment.

"Why did you hide so much from me?"

Zophie's swirling eyes crinkled as she smiled softly. "You already hated yourself for the things Alexander made you do." She brushed his hair back from his face. "You would not have survived a lifetime of all your burdens."

Peter glanced past the angel, heart seizing in his chest. He had a heart beat again thanks to Zophiel. He should be grateful, but he only felt betrayal. "Why? Why did you bind me?"

"Claire."

Ice slid down his spine as Zophiel faded.

"What does that mean?"

She was gone, and time unfroze. He leaped to his feet, scooping Rebecca up in his arms, feeding her healing magic as he carried her upstairs, steps growing sluggish as he went. She had used too much of her power—it was draining him fast.

He wondered if, like a moment ago, he could alter his actions in the memory. If he could change the past.

CHAPTER 14

Michael

Michael paced the room within the human dwelling he'd taken residence in since returning to Earth, grinding his teeth again. Hope had lodged itself in his chest, burrowing so deep it could scarcely be removed and yet... He'd let his guard down too soon. He'd dared to wish for a different world at the end of everything, but of course, evil still existed. As long as humans had the choice, there would be those who chose wrong.

It began with a bit of blood, but it would escalate as it had time and again in human history. Each time he or his siblings were tasked with ending a city so wicked there was no hope for redemption, a new one sprouted in its place.

Each time the seraphim were sent to teach the humans a lesson, years, sometimes only months passed before the lesson was forgotten. Now, when humanity was nearly extinct, and all that remained were those deemed good enough to live on, it had only taken a few weeks for them to shed blood.

"Michael?"

A dagger tore through him at the sound of her voice and he squeezed his eyes closed, praying she was a figment of his imagination. But no.

She was his eternal torment, and she existed both to complete his brother and to leave him irrevocably torn.

"Please look at me."

He should have ended it. Should have found the fountain and drunk from it. Why had he continued to live in misery when relief had been so near?

Featherlight fingers brushed his cheek, and he gasped at the contact, his piece of their soul stretching to meet it.

"I heard you saved a woman, and I thought... I hoped you might..."

Her touch evaporated, and slowly, he blinked his eyes open, taking her in. She was every bit as radiant as she had been the day she chose Raphael and buried a dagger in his chest for all eternity. Mesmerizing amber orbs searched his face, looking into his eyes, seeing beyond them to the fractured soul beneath—the piece she and Raphael had chosen not to bond with.

It was unnatural to have more than one soulmate. Of course, he hadn't expected her to choose them both, but—once—Michael had dared to believe *he* would be her choice. The hero who saved her from the fallen. The one who paid the greatest price so all humans would be free of Samael's reign on Earth.

But how could she? Who would want half a seraph for a mate? Unable to fly, unable to forget.

"Will you not speak to me?"

He was frozen, grasping desperately at the remains of his tattered soul, praying he would survive this encounter long enough to return to his home atop the mountain—to the fountain, to drink from it and finally put them all out of their misery.

She exhaled a slow breath. Honey and gardenia invaded his senses, sending a wave of bitter, tormented memories through him. Mary, in his arms, her tender lips pressed to his—her body warm against his as he carried her to a meadow near her family home. There, they lay on their backs staring up at the stars and he, drowning in all her sweet perfection, was lost, never to be recovered.

She leaned closer, and he jerked back, torn violently from the memories.

Pain ghosted over her face and she dipped her head, eyes downcast. "I'm sorry. I only meant to comfort you."

His being ached to touch her, to offer her what she desired. His soul strained against the confines of his rigid form, begging to give in and pull her close, but the spear lodged between his ribcage, buried deep, held him firmly in place.

When she looked up, meeting his gaze again, the depth of her sorrow struck him with such force he nearly staggered back.

She turned and fled the room.

When an hour passed, or a day, he roused from the agony he'd allowed himself to wallow in and moved to the doorway, leaning against it. Cool wood caressed his cheek, wiping away the memory of her touch, and a new ache settled in him.

Nothing existed for him now. In truth, he couldn't fathom why he had hung on so long. What had he been waiting for? Not his soul's analogous umbra, not redemption for the humans. What then? He moved on lead feet, kicking rocks and debris as he stumbled forward, desperate to reach his end and the sweet nothing that would follow.

"Michael? Where are you going?"

He halted. The human's voice, so unlike Mary's, sent a bolt of regret through him. He resumed walking, ignoring her. She would sway him from his path. Say or do something to encourage fledgling hope.

"Wait! I'll come with you."

His fingers flexed at his sides, as he picked up his pace, wishing not for the first time he could fly away from what came next. But his fate was to face all the hardships his brother never had.

Vassi moved faster than a human and in moments, strolled beside him. "I wanted to thank you. For saving me."

He continued along a cracked sidewalk, already overgrown with weeds, staring at the distant glittering spires of his home. Humans glanced up as he passed, eyes darting away when they spied his single wing. One or two openly gawked, their gazes burning into his scarred back, and he sped up.

"Sophia says I would be dead if not for you." Vassi's hand brushed his as she swung her arms beside him. He flinched away from her touch.

When he'd found her lying in a pool of her own blood, it wasn't disgust for the humans or anger he felt. It was a moment of blind terror at the thought of this world devoid of such a bright star. He'd thought of Mary as such a light once. The comparison sent another spasm of pain through him. Even now, disconnected as they were, he could sense his other half on this plane.

But she wasn't *his* anything, and he wasn't a half. Just as she and Raphael weren't complete without him.

"It's strange," Vassi continued, talking to herself, undeterred by his silence. "Ever since you saved me, I feel something," she rubbed her chest, "here."

Michael glanced sideways at her hand, rubbing over her breast-bone—where her soul lived.

"It is my healing magic." He looked away. "You were near death. A bit of your soul needed restoring, too."

Vassi walked beside him, silent, and he darted another quick look to his left. She bit her lower lip and scrunched her brows in confusion. Something in him lightened at her efforts to puzzle out his words. She looked up and her lips split into a dazzling smile.

A spasm struck him in the chest, making him gasp. Panic shot through him. If he hadn't already known who his soulmate was, he would have said the feeling was one of finding your other half. It wasn't. It was a fraction of what he felt in the mere presence of Mary, a drop in an ocean of longing, but it was... something.

Something he couldn't ignore.

CHAPTER 15

Peter

Was it because they'd talked about her or because Zophiel was somehow still directing his path, even at the end? Whatever the reason, he was in the passenger seat of Claire's car when his vision solidified on the next memory.

Her manic glee as she rounded a corner entirely too fast made him smile.

One of his favorite things about Claire was her ability to enjoy her life despite its cruelty.

If he was correct, she was seventeen, and this was the night she'd decided to make a break for it. He remembered the night going differently, but wasn't surprised in the least to learn it was another memory Zophiel had stolen. Dread pooled in his gut. It could mean only one thing. It would be another night he'd regret.

Claire downshifted as she tugged the wheel hard, the tires sliding over loose gravel around a sharp turn.

"Claire, could we slow down a bit?"

"Not a chance! Father will be back soon and I'm not letting any of those demons drag us back to that hell house. I'm getting you out of there for good." She winked, shifting again as she wedged her foot into the pedal and floored it on the straightaway.

Peter reached for the 'oh shit' handle overhead and ducked as they bounced over a pothole, the car seeming like it might rattle off its hinges.

"It's no use and you know it," he said. But he wasn't sure whether those were the words he'd said the first time this happened or if they were his—now.

She glanced over and his stomach dipped as her focus returned to the road, swerving around a curve at the last possible moment. "My father's not God. There must be a place beyond his reach."

Memories of a war several decades earlier swam in his mind. He should be grateful they weren't revisiting those; he would give anything not to relive the death of all those men. "You'd be surprised," he whispered.

Claire slowed as they approached a stop sign and an intersection. "Where are we going?"

She looked left, then right and turned right, flooring it once they turned onto the highway. "South. To Mexico. I've heard it's beautiful, and a dollar goes a long way."

Peter swallowed, reveling momentarily in the feeling of a throat working after spending so much time in the ether where no part of his body was material. He was certain he'd never been to Mexico. How far would they get? What would stop them? She was alive. She survived this, and that was all that mattered.

After several miles his grip loosened on the handhold, his shoulders slumping. He touched the radio dial, glancing at Claire. She nodded, and he spun it. A grin split her face as *I Can't Get Next to You* blared from the speakers and Claire started singing along at the top of her lungs.

He twisted the dial, turning the volume down. "Claire."

She stopped singing, grinning at him. "Yeah?"

"Why do you love sixties music so much?"

Her smile dropped, and the light in her eyes dimmed. "Mom."

Peter's breath caught in his throat. "You remember Sarah?"

She glanced at him again. "A little."

He was desperate to ask her more. None of the others had remembered their parents. But that wasn't true. Allie had some memories of Rachel.

"And she loved sixties music?"

Claire laughed. "You're going to think I'm silly."

He bumped his elbow against her ribs. "I already do."

That coaxed a smile back to her face. "Well, I have this one really specific memory. She wanted to join the Peace Corps, and a song came on the radio. I honestly don't even know what it was. I was probably four or five, but I remember, " Claire grinned, tucking a curl behind her ear. "She said, 'I'm so glad I had you. There weren't any radio stations in the place I was going and there's nothing like the music right now. I would have missed it if I didn't have you.'"

Claire's cheeks flamed. "I always thought she regretted me, but when I heard those words, I knew it wasn't true."

She looked up meeting his gaze, and something burned in his chest. It was Rebecca. Just as she had been in every other life, searching for love from even one of her parents. She'd wanted it so badly that she'd hung on to a memory from early childhood.

Peter lifted a hand, resting it over hers as his gaze met brilliant blue eyes. Even after all she'd endured, there was so much love in them.

A wobbling sensation jerked her attention to the road.

He felt it, but even with his preternatural speed, he couldn't stop the car from losing control.

Unbuckling his seatbelt, he dove across her lap, wrapping his body around hers and gripping the seat.

The car tipped, cracking as the world rolled over and over, metal scraping pavement each time it impacted the ground. Something rammed into his back and he squeezed her more tightly, cradling her neck and head in the crook of his shoulder.

The thin metal of the roof bent dangerously low and he reached for her seatbelt with one hand, unbuckling it as he tugged her down an instant before angry, groaning steel struck pavement and crumpled.

Millions of knives cut into his back, arms, and sides as the windshield became the most dangerous weapon in the vehicle.

Claire groaned in a long exaggerated sound as the world continued in slow motion. Then, all at once, it caught up with them.

The car bounced to a halt; the roof dented nearly to the dashboard, glass covering every surface, and slowly, Peter unwrapped himself from Claire's body. Every inch of him ached, but all his focus was on the precious girl wrapped in his battered arms.

Kicking hard against the door, he freed them from the vehicle and gingerly slid out, carefully tugging Claire with him.

Their eyes met and there was such terror in hers that, for a moment, he was frozen in panic. Her fragile body could be broken in a hundred ways.

"What hurts?" he whispered.

She inhaled a wet, ragged breath and screamed.

Peter's gaze left her face, trailing over her body, searching for the cause of her pain. Dark liquid pooled along the left side of her shirt, spreading quickly. He swore, setting her down softly on the grass and carefully lifted her shirt.

She gasped, hands going to her side, but he gently pushed them down, peeling wet fabric away from her skin. Under her left arm, crimson ran freely from some invisible wound and he tugged the shirt higher.

"Claire. Just wait. Wait. Breathe." Below her breast, a long thin bit of glass protruded from her ribcage. It was nestled between bone and most alarming were the tiny bubbles escaping around its edges.

"I'm going to help you," he said, holding up his hands. Cupping them, he whispered the words that had come naturally to him since the day Sarah had died. A dark, yellowish light burst from his fingers.

Claire's scream ripped through his soul. That wasn't right. He had forgotten in his panic that he wasn't Peter. He was Simon, twisted and vile, and his gifts were as well. Pulling his hands back in a panicked, jerky movement, he nearly gagged at the sight of Claire's black blood.

"I'm sorry. I'm sorry." The words tumbled from his mouth even as inky liquid bubbled from Claire's lips and her face went deathly white. "Claire. I... I don't know what to do." He tipped his forehead to hers and jumped when a shaky, icy hand brushed his cheek.

He leaned back watching a single tear streak down her face.

"It's..."

Pressing a finger to her lips, he shushed her. "Don't speak. It will only hurt." The words came out in a sob and he stared around the dark patch of highway, knowing no one was coming. No one would save her.

Gingerly, he lifted her head, terrified to move any part of her body, and cradled it in his lap. This couldn't be right. She wasn't dead. She had lived. She had Rachel and Robert. Had he changed the past somehow?

"Zophiel!"

Bright light flashed, and she appeared. He exhaled an unsteady breath. She would fix things. She would put it right.

"What's happened?" Zophiel asked, dropping to her knees beside him.

"Please help her. She's dying."

The angel glanced down at the black bubbling blood still leaking from her side. "What have you done?"

"I tried to heal her. I forgot. I forgot."

"Shhh, I'm here," Zophiel said. "Claire, can you hear me?" Claire's eyes, wide with shock, didn't register her words, staring blankly at nothing over his shoulder. "You've poisoned her. I can mend this, but there will be a scar."

A hysterical laugh bubbled up Peter's chest. "Who cares about a scar?"

"Not a physical scar. One on her soul."

"But she'll live?"

Zophiel pursed her lips. "I can save her. Not without great cost."

"Whatever it is, I'll pay it."

"It's not your payment to make."

He frowned down at the girl whose breaths came in shorter and shorter bursts. "Just do it. Hurry."

Zophiel nodded. "He won't like this, but what choice is there?" She said the words as if to herself and cupped her hands over the wound. "When I tell you, pull the glass free. Are you ready?"

He nodded, lifting a shaking hand, and pinched the glass between two fingers.

"Now."

He pulled, and it slid free, followed by a slow trickle of dark blood. It wasn't all black and something in his chest loosened.

Zophiel murmured softly as white light erupted from her fingers. Deep in his soul, he knew that was what it was meant to look like. Not the stained, yellow magic leaking from his palms.

Claire sucked in a sharp, clear breath and all his focus returned to her.

"Claire. You're alright."

Her eyes cleared, gaze darting to the angel hovering over her then to Peter. A soft smile played on her lips and he thought he would break in that moment. She was alive, and she was staring at him like nothing and no one else mattered in the world.

When Zophiel had healed his wounds, she produced a stone from her pocket. "You'll need this," she said, handing it to him.

He looked down, then back at Claire who was searching the wreckage for her purse.

"What did it cost her?"

Zophiel's sad eyes met his. "She will die like this. Not in this life; in another. In one of her brief lives, she'll die at seventeen, choking on her own blood."

Peter felt the shock of that revelation to his bones. Everyone had accused Alexander's demon of killing Allie, but it hadn't been him. "Is it because of my twisted magic?" The words were a whisper.

Zophiel's lips pressed into a thin line. "These were the truths I tried to shield you from. To give your soul a chance to find the right path."

He stood, backing away from her. "Is that a yes?"

The sorrowful expression painted across her face was too much.

"Get me out of this memory. Take it back. I don't want it."

She stood, brushing off satin white robes. "It doesn't work like that, Peter. You'll have to face these demons to determine where you end the journey."

He was thrust like a punch to the gut from the memory. The absolute nothing that enveloped him was a momentary reprieve from the torrent of emotions raging through him. But even in this place where emotion did not exist, one thought raced through his mind over and over.

My fault. My fault Allie died.

CHAPTER 16

Sophia

The Naphil had some nerve showing up in her town, acting as though she were better than the rest of them simply because of her half-angelic blood. If Sophia had learned anything these many months among angels, it was that they might be strong, but they were imperfect—just like everyone else.

"Sister, this is Leah's best friend and one of the night creatures who saved the humans from all demon kind. Perhaps you should show her more respect."

Helena's gaze swiveled to her brother. "Night being? Like Lysander? Was he not cast into Primoria for becoming such a creature?"

Aniel reached for Helena, pulling her to his side. He gazed intently at her, and Sophia knew at once the mated pair was speaking mind-to-mind. She had seen it often enough with Leah and Gabriel. The thought of her best friend twisted something in her chest. They had left days before and she wasn't sure when she would see them again. The ache of missing her best friend was sharp. She'd even take Gabriel's grumpy brooding if it meant Leah came back right now.

Though they all had a part to play at the end of the world, Sophia could have done without Helena. She may be related to the Graves family, but she was nothing like them. And nothing like Aesop, who had proved himself more than capable since arriving on the mortal plane.

His sister, who'd scarcely been seen except at mealtimes, refused to adopt the common language the town had voted to use, and had yet to take part in any chores. As far as Sophia could tell, she was a spoiled brat who expected others to serve her every whim.

"We're planning a scouting party to find Cassia and the rest of the missing souls," Zadkiel said to Sophia. "Will you join us?"

"Do you not need me in town to protect the people against potential demon attacks?"

"Your mother and the other witches have proven themselves capable in a fight. The other night creatures will also be here to lend a hand."

Sophia glanced at Helena and Aniel, still locked in their silent conversation. "Who is going on this expedition?"

"Only those who can fly or move quickly."

She nodded. *Good.* If they'd said the princess was coming along, she would have been inclined to pass, even if it meant she would not be the one to find Cassia.

"You'll need to bring food. It is scarce beyond the town," Aniel said, stepping away from Helena.

After Sophia had gathered supplies for an extended trip, she'd met with Aniel, Zadkiel, and several other seraphim. The plan was simple: start in town and move in different directions, scouring every inch of land until they reached the ocean. She would take the heavily wooded area leading south with little visibility from the sky.

Her route held many caves which had already been searched, but if Cassia and her group were smart, they wouldn't stay in one place long, meaning she'd need to check them again. Luckily for Sophia, Cassia was the only night being among those left in Sheol, so they couldn't have gone far.

"Sophia!" She looked up to see one of General Vaughn's men approaching, waving a hand overhead. "Wait!" The man stopped, red faced and panting. "General Vaughn asked me to bring you this." He slapped a plastic walkie-talkie into her palm. A light on top glowed red.

"Does it work?"

The man straightened. "Yep. Works within fifty miles. Ideally. If you need help or see anything worth mentioning, push this." He pointed to a black button atop the device. "And talk into it."

She pressed her thumb down. "Testing."

Static crackled before Angeliki's voice rang out. "I hear you. Be careful, Pythia."

"I will, Mama. Take care of yourself while I'm gone. If you see Cassia, don't go near her."

"Don't worry about me, child. I was a woman grown before Cassia was born."

Sophia smiled, sliding the clip of her new walkie-talkie into the band of her pants. "Do any of the angels have one?"

"No ma'am. The creatures looked like their heads might explode when we tried convincing them to bring devices. It's just you."

Sophia shook her head. Of course, the stubborn beings hadn't agreed to something so *human*. Bidding the soldier farewell, she tightened the strap of her pack and darted into the forest; the darkness enveloped her, humidity clinging to her skin—a welcome change from the brittle dry air in the mountains.

In this ancient forest, surrounded by the might of Mother Nature, peacefulness stole over her.

Her gift rose, humming under her skin. These weeks on Earth, among the elements, with her gift restored, had made her begin to feel a little like herself again.

A branch cracked in the distance and her senses came alive. Since the world had ended, she'd seen or heard no signs of fauna. Only her kind, the angels, and the demons had survived; that or the animals were hiding. She reached out with the water magic, the easiest way to tell if another witch was nearby. Nothing. But if it was Cassia, she would not sense her gift. That made her even more dangerous. Sophia stopped beside the trunk of a massive spruce and scanned the late afternoon sun-dappled forest for any sign of the thing responsible for the noise. All was still and silent. She spun in a slow circle, gaze catching on the shadows of swaying leaves.

A crack sounded—farther away this time—and she darted after it on light feet.

She slowed when she reached the mouth of a wide cave set among a heavily wooded part of the forest. It was eerily quiet and the hairs on the back of her neck rose as she crept closer to the entrance.

Something brushed the wall inside the cave. Sophia froze. Cautiously, she inched toward the darkness within, breath trapped in her chest as she listened for another sound.

A crash echoed from somewhere inside. Sophia stumbled back, narrowly missing sharp antlers as a stag charged her, racing out of the cave and darting away. Sophia held a hand to her chest, catching her breath. A deer! And if there was a deer, there must be other animals still alive. Perhaps the winter wouldn't be so bleak.

Lifting the radio to her mouth, she pressed the button down. "Mama! There are animals in the forest. I saw a deer!"

She released the button, waiting for her mother's reply. A crack sounded against her skull and she had a moment to wonder who or what had struck her before the world went dark.

CHAPTER 17

Peter

With quiet resignation, Peter stepped into his next memory as though striding through a door.

The blaring horn of a New York City cab made him stagger backward, heart racing. He pressed his hand to his thumping chest. This was a recent memory. After he'd become a reash.

Moving along the street, with no idea where he'd been headed, he glanced down at his phone. *I'm still not sure*, the text read. His heart warmed. It was a text from Allie. All at once, he knew what this memory would be.

He picked up speed, crossing an intersection as a black Mercedes G-Wagon pressed on the gas, actively working to run him down; despite it, he smiled. He fucking loved New York.

Peter tugged at his collar and ducked into an alley. She'd sent that message six hours before she boarded a plane and set off for college in Boston.

Allie loved surprises, and what better surprise than this?

Lifting his phone to his ear, he confirmed the reservation for their suite and tucked it back in his pocket. Taking the stairs two at a time, he swiped the access panel beside the door and stepped through.

"Good morning, Mr. Carey." He dipped his chin to Elaine, the firm's office manager, and strode through the reception area to his desk.

Sliding into his chair, custom designed by his good friend Brad Ford, he sighed, loosening his tie. This memory was a gift, a reprieve from the horrible truth waiting in that distant past. Who would have guessed he'd miss work of all things?

A knock at the door had him looking up. "Hey. Can we talk?"

He exhaled a slow breath, dropping his gaze to the papers atop his desk. "Can it wait, Valentina? I have a lot on my plate this morning and I'm leaving for Boston in a few."

Heels clacked over cork wood floors as she came into the room, sitting across from him. "Simon."

He shuffled papers on his desk, not really looking at them.

"Simon, look at me."

He looked up, raising a brow.

Valentina's shining crimson lips formed a pout. "I'm worried about you."

He huffed a laugh. "There's no need to be concerned."

"I don't mean I'm worried for your safety. I mean, I'm worried she'll hurt you... Again."

He studied her, noting the lines creasing the corners of her eyes and the puffiness cleverly hidden by thick liner. She had been crying. "Val. We've talked about it. I'm sorry, I really am, but you know how I feel. I never lied to you."

She leaned forward, cleavage bursting from a shirt with too many buttons undone. "I know what you said, but we were happy, baby. For a long time. People don't just throw that away."

He pushed against his desk, chair rolling backward before he stood, going to the door to close it. Spinning around, he faced her. "I know I hurt you. You weren't expecting any of it, but it was six years ago. You have to move on."

Hurt flashed over her face, quickly replaced by anger. "She's a child. It's gross."

He ran a hand over his face. "She's older than I am."

"She doesn't know that. Maybe I should call her and remind her. It never does seem to work out between you and Rebecca."

Cold fury sliced through him, but he stuffed his hands into his pockets. "We both know you won't. Now get out."

Valentina stood, putting a little too much sway into her movement as she approached, closing the distance between them.

He stepped aside, and she moved with him, pressing herself against his chest. "She'll forget you again, but I never will. Don't think I'll wait around to pick up the pieces when she crushes your heart into dust."

Peter nodded. "I hope you don't for me, Val. I want you to find someone who makes you happy."

She raised a hand and, for a moment, he thought she'd slap him. But she backed up. "You'll call. When she breaks your heart. You always do."

She sauntered out of his office, without looking back, and he closed the door, leaning against it as he sighed heavily.

With each memory, he seemed to be more present and less of an observer. It hadn't gone quite like that the first time, but somehow he'd had enough control to say the things he had wanted to when she last came into his office. A weight lifted from his chest—guilt he'd been carrying.

He pulled his phone out of his pocket, scrolled to Allie's name, and typed out a quick reply. *I'm proud of you. No second thoughts.*

Somehow, the message he'd never sent—the one he would have if things had gone the way they did this time—allowed the text to go through. Another burden lifted. She wouldn't have been so upset when he arrived to surprise her. Perhaps these memories were a chance to do things differently. Perhaps at the end of the world, he would find her and things would go differently.

CHAPTER 18

Helena

Helena swiped her hand against her forehead. This wasn't supposed to be how the end of the world went. She was supposed to go to heaven. To spend eternity with her angel. Her other half.

"Dig the holes deeper, Sister. At that depth, the seed will be uncovered at the first rain."

She scowled at her younger brother. What gave him the right to supervise her? The night creature who had stayed behind to guard them, Vassi, darted by, her movements so quick she was a blur. An angel followed at the same speed. Helena wasn't sure, but it looked like he may have only had one wing.

She frowned. Why did he get to stay when Aniel was forced to leave with the others?

"Look, you can't make the dirt so compact so the seed can't breathe," Aesop said, and Helena's gaze snapped to her brother.

She shot to her feet, wiping dirty palms on her tunic. "If I'm doing such a poor job of it, perhaps my skills lie elsewhere."

Aesop's brow dipped, and the expression reminded her painfully of Lysander. His hair wasn't quite the same shade, his jaw not as chiseled as the brother who turned heads wherever he went back in Athens,

76

but those dark lashes and piercing eyes were the Gavras eyes if ever she had seen them. When they had all shared a roof, she would have said Lysander was her most annoying brother, but she would give anything for a last goodbye. What had become of him? Was he some deformed, demonic creature, as Aniel said they became after so long in the dark? Had he been slain by the angels?

"You're right, Sister. I believe you can best help the ladies managing sewing and mending."

Making clothes? Helena didn't know the first thing about the task, but it meant escaping the dirt and mud and a chance to influence the style in her new village. A welcome change.

Helena peeked under her lashes at the elderly matrons and... *men* encircling a pile of fabrics. They had a list of measurements, requests, and priorities. At the top was stitching canvas to gather and filter rainwater for the crops.

Not a glamorous task, but she welcomed the warmth of the fire and the company of others.

The woman to her right handed her a set of knitting needles and thick wool. When she spoke, Helena's brows knitted, and she shook her head, failing to understand the foreign tongue. A man beside her spoke in the same strange language, and Helena sighed. Perhaps this, too, would be a lonely task.

A shrill sound roused Helena from her work. She glanced around as the others stood, murmuring to one another and shuffled toward the door. Helena stood, stretching her back. There was quiet contentment in the work and the buzz of voices, though incomprehensible, made the day pass quickly.

Everyone formed a line along a set of low tables and began moving. When it was her turn, she picked up a dish, as she'd learned to do here in Colorado, and held it out for a serving. She found a place to sit, sliding beside several people stuffed on a bench.

None of the faces were familiar, and she felt a pang of longing for Aniel or even her brother. Those who worked in the garden ate first so they could return to their labor, then the guards. Her group came last, their work deemed less important and so their rations were fewer. She knew it made sense, but the thought that anyone's contribution was greater than another's chafed.

When her belly was full, she moved to the sink in the corner, rinsing her dish and scrubbing it clean. She set it beside several others to dry overnight and stepped outside into the rapidly chilling air. The weather in this place was an adjustment she was trying and failing to acclimate to. A shiver racked her, and she wrapped her arms around herself.

With no way of knowing when Aniel would return and no way to reach their room without him, she glanced along the paved path, biting her lip. Should she knock on someone's door? Ask for a bed and a blanket? Would they understand her?

"Are you lost, dear?"

Helena spun around, nearly crying in relief at hearing someone speak her mother tongue. The woman was beautiful, about her age, with her hair cut short like a man's.

"Yes," she breathed. "I have nowhere to stay and I know no one."

"Come with me, child." The woman held out her hand, and Helena took it, exhaling a long sigh. Her fingers ached where they had gripped the needles and shook in her hold. "Please, what should I call you?"

The woman smiled, "I am Xenia, but everyone calls me Yia-Yia."

Helena glanced at the woman's smooth hands, wrapped tightly around hers. "Surely not. You are no grandmother."

Yia-Yia tugged her forward and pushed open the red door she'd seen before. They stepped through the doorway into a home warmed by a crackling fire and Helena glanced around nervously at a room full of women reclining in chairs or beside the fire. They eyed her as she entered, and she squeezed Yia-Yia's hand, halting.

Yia-Yia glanced back and pulled her inside. "Ladies," she said. "I have brought us a lost lamb."

Several women sat up. Their gazes moved over her clothing and hair, trailing to her sandal-clad feet, but none of their looks were unfriendly.

"What's your gift?" someone asked in crudely spoken Greek.

Helena released Yia-Yia's hand. "I possess all four elemental gifts."

Murmurs around the room grew louder, and a woman stood. "Prove it. I wield fire and water."

Helena thrust a hand out, sending sparks into the fireplace. Drawing water from a woman's cup, she formed a ball in the air, letting it hover for several seconds before it splashed to the floor.

The challenger grumbled as she stepped out of the puddle and some women frowned. Helena swallowed. She had to remember she was not in Athens anymore—she was not from a well-respected family here. If she hoped to find a place among the only women who were anything like her, she would have to play nice.

"I apologize. It has been centuries since I wielded my gift."

The women's faces softened and Helena's shoulders relaxed.

"Show me air," another woman said from across the room and Helena felt the strength of her gift. In this moment, she had an overwhelming desire to show her up, to prove her might, but she would not win them over by being boastful. She twisted one finger, curling an invisible current of wind around it and let it dissipate slowly.

The witch dipped her chin in approval.

Helena swiveled her gaze around the room, awaiting her final test.

"You must be tired, child, Yia-Yia said. "Come with me. I'll show you to a bed."

Helena inhaled sharply. No last test? A memory of Sanura's test—her coven's harsh and swift punishment for those who failed—sprang to mind. Was Sanura fearful of repercussions had she not tricked the coven into believing she was one of them? Yet these witches had threatened no retribution and hadn't even tested all four elements before offering refuge in their home.

They weren't Nephilim. Surely three gifts were enough to grant her the privilege of sleeping among them.

"This bed was set aside for Cassia." Yia-Yia handed her a soft blanket, made of a material Helena had never experienced before, and she took it, dipping her head.

Yia-Yia's eyes held a grief Helena had seldom seen in another and she felt the woman's sadness keenly. "Cassia is the night being the angels are searching for?"

She nodded, gaze dropping to the floor.

Helena reached for her, wrapping her in a tight embrace. "Pray they find her and bring her back unharmed."

Yia-Yia looked up, warmth shining in her ancient eyes. "I wish for nothing less, child."

CHAPTER 19

Peter

Peter pulled up outside the Logan International Airport and reached across to the passenger seat, lifting the flowers he'd had time to pick up on the way now that Valentina hadn't wasted so much of his morning.

He stepped out onto the sidewalk, and a smile crept onto his face when he spied her approaching. He reached the exit door before she did and held it open.

She looked up, gasping, and squealed. "You're here!" Throwing her arms around him, her bags toppled to the ground, and he tugged her into a tight embrace, inhaling her scent. It had been so long since he'd held her like this and another bit of the heaviness weighing on him lightened with *her* in his arms.

"Did you think I'd leave you to handle your first day on your own?" he breathed into her hair.

She hugged him tighter. "No. I knew you'd come."

Far too soon, he leaned back, taking in her normal eyes, and held up the flowers. "For you."

Her lips parted in a dazzling smile and she took them, glancing around at her bags. "I don't have enough hands."

Peter stepped around her, lifting her bag onto his shoulder and grabbing her suitcase handle. "Come on. I want to show you the city before orientation."

She wrapped her coat tightly around her and his chest warmed, knowing the reminder text he'd sent about the weather was a good call. It might even save them from the fight he knew was coming.

The memory raced ahead, and he braced himself, expecting it to halt at the coffee shop, where the argument began.

Instead, his vision solidified outside her school. Allie was sucking in air, struggling to get her breathing under control.

"What did she do to me?" she asked.

He rubbed circles on her back. This was the moment he'd encouraged her to go back inside, and everything had changed. If Sophia hadn't been her friend, she wouldn't have unbound her memories.

The words hovered on the tip of his tongue. He should tell her to go in, to ignore the witch, but this was his memory, and he's already learned he could alter it. All he had to do now was tell her to leave, to walk away and forget college. They could have their time together.

She looked up, meeting his eyes. "Simon?"

"She's a witch. A powerful one. I'm worried for your safety."

Hairs along the back of his neck rose, and he glanced around as he felt the pressure of a time bubble envelop him.

Zophiel appeared.

His brow furrowed. "I know you weren't here before."

"What are you doing, Peter?" she asked. "You're not supposed to change things. You're only supposed to observe."

He crossed his arms, eyes narrowing as he stared up at the glowing creature. "Why not? Why can't I change it? I'm dead. It's over. This is my chance to steal back the happiness I lost. The happiness I waited a century for."

"That's not how it works. You're not here to carve out a new life."

"No? What am I here for, Zoph? Torture? Punishment? I've had enough of that."

As if the words broke her spell, time resumed and Zophiel faded away.

Allie rubbed her arms. "Really? So you think I'm not safe?"

"No. Come on. I got us a hotel room. Let's go back there and decide what to do next."

Allie nodded, so much hope and trust in her eyes. She held out a hand, and he took it, leading her back to her car.

"Hey! Wait up!"

Sophia's lilting accented voice cut through the night, and Allie's grip tightened on his.

"What do we do?"

"Ignore her," he said, tugging her at a faster pace.

"Alexandra, please! I need your help!"

Allie halted, pulling her hand from his. "Maybe I should hear her out."

Peter turned to face her, seeing Sophia running after them. "She's a witch. You can't trust her."

Allie's brow creased, her mouth dipping into a frown. "You said I'm a witch. Does that mean you can't trust me?"

"No, Allie. That's not—"

"I'm so glad I caught up with you," Sophia said, panting. She pressed a hand into her side and inhaled a long breath. "You guys were so fast."

Allie spun around. "My boyfriend says you're a witch and that you'll hurt us. Is that true? Are you going to hurt us?"

Sophia's gaze darted to him, a dark cloud of emotion rolling across her face. "Me?" She snorted. "Why would I hurt you? I need your help to save the world."

CHAPTER 20

Michael

"Vassi."

Vassi spun around. "I need to find my sisters. I know you don't care about them, but they're all I have."

"They aren't all you have." Michael bit down hard on his tongue, tasting blood. Why had he said those words? They couldn't be further from the truth. She was nothing to him, and he was certainly nothing to her.

She searched his face, and he was frozen, waiting for the judgment, the pity that always flooded their faces. Instead, he saw only hope, and that withered his already shriveled soul more than any condemnation. He looked away, casting his gaze to the tree line behind their little town.

A tentative hand rose. He tracked the movement in his periphery but didn't turn toward it. Her fingers found his jaw, tracing the line of smooth skin and turning it to face her. Her eyes met his—rich mahogany refracting the light of a fading sun, and her lips tipped up in a playful grin.

His chest lurched in response.

"Is there another who claims to be mine?"

For the briefest instant, he let her hold him in her thrall, captured by her aura, so alive and warm, before he jerked away from her touch. "If there is, perhaps you should seek him out."

"Have I not?"

Her words caught him by surprise. He'd meant to spurn her, to tarnish her pride. It had taken less to wound Mary. But Vassi was made of stronger stuff and she met his stony stare with a challenge in her eyes. How long had it been since any had dared to look him in the eye and not shrink from his fury? Gabriel. He was the one exception. Yet even he rarely tempted Michael's wrath. This bold creature showed no signs of backing down.

"I am spoken for."

Vassi's eyebrows shot up. "By whom? I see no one here to claim you."

He opened his mouth, but she closed the distance between them, sucking his bottom lip between her teeth and biting down, drawing blood. The act of sharing blood was reserved for soulmates, and his soul pulsed a rapid thrum in response to his terror and elation.

His arms came around her, tugging her against him possessively. A fervor he'd never known waged war inside him, battling his self-control. She slid her tongue between his teeth, finding his and daring it to join in their dance.

He groaned, tightening his grip, and sucked hard on the tongue, brazenly exploring his mouth. Fingers found his hair, nails scraping over his scalp and coiling in his curls. She yanked hard, making his hips grind involuntarily against the woman pressed into his growing desire.

It had been a millennium since the thought of a woman's touch had entered his mind. Not since... He shoved the idea away, unwilling to allow her memory to taint the moment. His hands trailed south, and he cupped the swell of her ass, groaning again at the firmness of it.

Vassi pressed against him and he lifted, taking her weight. She responded eagerly, wrapping her legs around his waist, fingers pulling harder at his hair as she devoured his mouth. Never had a woman been so forward in her need; his body came alive in response.

He walked her toward the home he had been occupying, kicking the door wide and pressing her against a wall in his sitting room. She grunted on impact and ground her hips against his hard length, sucking his lip between her teeth to bite down once more.

Without thought, he reciprocated, teeth slicing into her full bottom lip. Warm coppery liquid filled his mouth, trickling down his throat and, with it, Vassi's life force. He tasted it as it swam in his veins and settled inside him. Where the dark corners of his being resided, light filtered through, purging the shadows and making him feel whole. He had never exchanged blood with his soulmate, only kisses, but if he had, he imagined it would have felt something like this.

Michael released Vassi, shuddering, and stumbled back.

She dropped heavily to her feet, shaking herself from the same fevered daze he'd been in.

He looked her up and down, cataloging very human imperfections. The faint aura surrounding her spoke of a diluted bloodline. She was not Nephilim; even if she had been, he had a soulmate, and it wasn't her. This was... wrong.

"Get out."

Vassi's mouth dropped open. The challenge in her eyes remained, though, and she straightened. "No."

He scoffed. "Don't you know a dismissal when you hear one? I said leave."

Vassi tugged at the corner of her threadbare shirt, pulling it down, to cover the marks beginning to bloom on her hips where he'd gripped her tightly. They would be dark tomorrow, but some of his healing energy still coursed through her. He had tasted it in her blood. She would heal quickly enough.

"I know a scared man when I see one and his cowardice won't chase me away."

It was Michael's turn to gape at the creature who had dared to speak to him with such insolence. "You think too highly of yourself. I am no man."

Vassi pushed off the wall, doing the unthinkable and closing the distance between them. "I know your type. You think you have a monopoly on grief? That you're the only one the world has tried to destroy? I have news for you, *Michael*." The way she said his name made him stiffen. "You're not special." She pressed closer until their noses were nearly touching. "When you've gotten over yourself, come find me."

She pushed past him, knocking him aside as she strode confidently for the door. If he couldn't taste emotion—didn't know with one-hundred percent certainty she meant those words—he would have guessed it was her defense mechanism. Her way of deflecting his cruelty.

But the witch wasn't hurt or shamed. She was angry. Angry with him? He shook his head. It didn't matter. He wasn't a creature to lie with another out of carnal desire or base need. The sins of the flesh were for those of weaker constitution. Only once, in his long existence had he ever done so—before he met his soulmate—and he would not make that mistake again.

Why, then, did the thrum of his soul race at the thought of her anger?

CHAPTER 21

Peter

Peter grabbed Allie's hand, pulling her toward the car. "Come on, she's using magic to muddle your brain. Let's go before she traps you in a spell."

Allie yanked her hand free. "You know, you told me a lot of things today and I accepted them, but telling me that other witches are bad but I'm not, I draw the line there."

Sophia stepped closer, smiling viciously at Peter before her gaze moved back to Allie. "It's so good to find a sister on campus and you're so powerful. I could feel your energy from across the courtyard."

Allie's lips tipped up and Peter could tell Sophia was already winning her over.

"Really? What did it feel like?" Allie asked. "I just found out I'm a witch. I can't believe I met another one so quickly."

Sophia cupped her palm, forming a small bubble of water. "Water is my most powerful element. I can sense when anyone else has it. And you definitely have it."

Allie beamed at her, then glanced back at Peter. "Isn't it lucky I found someone who can help me?"

Peter stretched out his hand. "Allie, if you've ever trusted me, please trust me now. She isn't a good person."

Allie's smile faltered, and her gaze moved between the two of them.

Sophia's eyes narrowed. "Oh really. And you are to be trusted."

"What does that mean?" Allie asked, brows furrowing in confusion.

"He's a night creature. They steal souls."

Allie's hand flew to her hip, but some of her resolve was already cracking, indecision warring on her face. He'd told her he was something evil. She'd guessed a vampire, but the truth was worse and Sophia was right. He did steal souls—drained them from demons and, occasionally, humans.

What was he doing? What was he playing at, attempting to recreate moments in a fictional past when none of it was true and never would be? "She's right."

Sophia swiveled her gaze to his. "I am?"

"She is?" Allie sounded like she'd hoped it wasn't true even if she had already come to the same conclusion.

"Yes. I'm not a good person." Peter said. "I'm not even a person. Sophia will show you just how awful I've been." He faced Sophia. "There's an obscura spell on her memories, placed there by angels, but I helped. Go ahead, Sophia. Remove it."

Both girls gaped at him, but Sophia squinted and her mouth fell open. "He's right."

She pressed her thumb to Allie's forehead, shoving her backward.

Peter didn't need to remain in this memory to know what came next.

CHAPTER 22

Sophia

Sophia blinked, groaning around the ache in her temple. Slowly, her vision came into focus and she took in the striation along jutting stone walls that disappeared into darkness. Glancing down, she swore, yanking against chains she'd never expected to see again, and certainly not at the end of the world.

Ice shot through her. It wasn't possible. Sanura was gone. She had seen it with her own eyes.

Pushing onto her feet, she wedged the toe of her boot against the wall and pulled. It was no use. Her bonds were spelled just as they had been all those times Sanura had trapped her. How? After nearly everything was destroyed, how had someone gotten the manacles used to hold her and the other witches?

Of course, her walkie-talkie was gone and her recent message to base camp would mean no one wondered where she was for some time. A chill hung in the air, the dampness soaking into her bones. Since the realms had collided, her human aches and discomforts had returned; deep inside this cave, she might freeze if she had to spend the night without a coat or fire for warmth. How she missed the ability to wrap herself in a protective bubble against the elements.

"Hello?!" It was a risk—altering her captors that she was awake—but it was better to know who had taken her than allow the fear of the unknown to consume her. When she was alive, she'd clung to the hope of eternity, and after she became a night creature, she no longer feared death. But now, when there was no afterlife, the consequences of someone's vile actions would be permanent.

A shudder rolled through her. "Is anyone there?!" Sophia's voice cracked, and she worked to tamp down the tremble.

Rocks skittering over packed earth from deep inside the cave made her jump, and she swiveled her head, peering into the inky distance. The sound came again. From the darkness, the outline of a person appeared. She knew at once it was a man and her heart slowed. *Not Sanura.*

He was of average height, in strange clothes from another time, and had a beard that desperately needed shaving. He stepped into the light, stopping several feet away from Sophia. "She's not here, but she'll be back," he said. "Try nothing. Those chains won't open for anyone but their owner."

Another spike of fear shot through Sophia. Who was *she*? "I'm thirsty. Do you have any water?"

The man cocked a sandy eyebrow. "Water's the only thing we *do* have on this forsaken planet."

Sophia worked to muster a smile, but none came. Despite the cold, a trickle of sweat ran down her back. She inhaled through her nose, exhaling slowly to calm her racing heart. "Could I have a cup?"

Without a word, the man turned and disappeared into the yawning darkness of the cave.

She swallowed thickly, leaning against the wall. Logically, she knew there was nothing to do but wait, but trapped in these bindings—in another cave—held by some mysterious woman, her thoughts raced back to those lonely nights when things seemed bleak.

As her eyes adjusted, she made out shapes deeper within the recesses and spied several boxes that looked to be military grade. She squinted, trying to make out the words printed along the sides, but they were covered by tarps and shadow and she could only read a few letters. AMM.

A silhouette from farther inside the cave appeared, and in moments, the man from before returned with a tin cup in hand. "Attempt nothing foolish or you'll get nothing else from me."

Sophia nodded, holding out her shackled hands. He inched forward, stretching the cup toward her and she moved slowly, wrapping her fingers around cold metal. "Thank you."

He backed up quickly. It was clear he was aware how dangerous she was, even with her magic bound by chains. Whoever had her knew what she was capable of.

"Ah, you're awake."

Sophia spun, liquid sloshing over the side of her cup as she turned. Cassia. It couldn't be. Surely her sister wasn't behind the kidnapping. Her heart sank.

Cassia's wicked grin made Sophia's stomach twist as she moved into the cave with the carcass of a deer slung over her shoulder.

"Cassia. Why?"

Cassia's smile fell as she strode past Sophia and dropped the stag at the man's feet. "Pierre, get a fire started and tell the others to help skin and cook it. Equal portions for all."

The man—Pierre—nodded, bending to grab the dead animal's legs and drag it away.

Cassia turned slowly, taking her time to face Sophia again. Her gaze roved over Sophia's thin sweater and pants. "You won't last the night in those clothes. Up here on the mountain, it gets cold."

"What do you want from me?"

"It's not what I want *from* you," Cassia said. "It's what I want you *for*."

The ice in Sophia's veins leeched up her arms, stretching to her fingertips. "What do you mean?"

Cassia reached inside her coat, looping her fingers around a gold chain and producing an oval-shaped amulet with a crescent moon carved along the face.

Sophia backed up, shoulder bumping against jagged stone as she moved to get as far from it as possible. "That thing is useless now. Why carry it with you?" As she said the words, some of her conviction faltered. What if she was wrong? What if Sanura had escaped Sheol with the rest of them?

"It's my turn to ask questions, *Sister.*" The word was said with enough malice that Sophia could not mistake Cassia's meaning. "Where's Peter? What have you done with him?"

Sophia's brow furrowed and her shoulders relaxed. "I haven't seen Peter since I left Sheol."

Cassia darted forward, pressing her nose to Sophia's. "Liar! He left Sheol moments before the rest of us. I've found everyone else. Everyone who's still alive. You have him. I know you do."

Sophia lifted her bound hands, wiping spittle from her cheek. "Is that what truly brought you to camp? If you searched the houses, you know he wasn't there."

A muscle under Cassia's eye jumped and her too wide eyes swiveled left, toward the darkness. Sophia strained to hear whatever had caught her sister's attention, but could make out nothing beyond the rustling of leaves and the wind picking up speed.

"You can either tell me where you're keeping him or stay here and risk the elements until I've searched every inch of your camp. It might take days." Cassia leaned back, lifting nails sharpened to points to examine them. "How long do you think you can survive in temperatures that dip below freezing each night?"

Sophia swallowed, heart jumping erratically in her chest. She wasn't kept updated on everything the angels did, but if they had found Peter, she would have heard of it. If Cassia intended to keep her until she found him, there was no end to this new hell.

"He's in the bunker." She schooled her face into neutrality as Cassia's face lit up in triumph. "But you'll never find him on your own. Take me with you."

Her sister's hand moved so fast that Sophia had no time to dodge it. A crack sounded in her ears as she was flung backward. Her head hit something sharp, and she slumped to the ground, dazed. Her vision darkened, and she sucked in a shallow breath around the pulsing beat of blood pounding in her skull.

Cassia crouched beside her, leaning close to whisper in her ear. "Don't ever lie to me again."

She stood, backing out, and in moments was gone.

CHAPTER 23

Peter

When Peter left the void to enter his next memory, he knew at once something was wrong. Where he'd been solid—corporeal—in the other memories, this time he could see the mortal plane but felt nothing. He had no body, no mouth from which to speak. He wondered if it meant he was inching toward his final death.

He was in his apartment in New York. It was dark, unlived in. Outside his fortieth-floor window, thick snowfall obscured the view more than he'd ever seen in New York. He wanted to see out and—as if his thoughts controlled this memory—he was at the window, peering down. Below, a blanket of white covered the Earth.

Behind him, the door buzzed. He faced it as it cracked open, and Valentina stepped inside. She looked older. Tired. This was recent, but if he wasn't here, what sort of memory could it be?

She closed the door, flipping on a light. "Simon?"

He listened, waiting for a reply that never came.

She moved into his apartment, removed her shoes, and padded to the kitchen. She flipped the switch, scanned the space, and opened the refrigerator. He watched over her shoulder as she slid items aside, lifting an old take-out box and sniffing it. Wrinkling her nose, she set it back down and shut the refrigerator.

She left the kitchen and stepped into his room, turning on lights as she went. His bed was neatly made, the down comforter stretched tight over a king-sized bed centered in an immaculate room. He could smell nothing, but if that sense had come with him, he was certain the scent of cleaning products would be heavy in the air.

Beside the window, a white vase, taken from his old room at the Graves estate, was filled with lavender, but the petals were shriveled and dead. The house cleaner never touched his flowers. Even if she'd come this week, she wouldn't have removed them.

They were the only sign it had been some time since Peter had been there. But he'd moved to his apartment after leaving Valentina. That meant this was after he had gone with Sanura and the witches. But how long?

"Astaroth."

Peter's attention snapped to Valentina. She had settled herself on the bed, running a hand over the comforter, and closed her eyes. Some time must have passed without his notice in this strange in-between state. Now she wore a silk nightgown, but he hadn't seen her change. She was sitting up, blankets thrown back. Black lines ran down her cheeks.

The demon appeared in the room and Peter hissed, trying to lunge for him, but only moved a few feet closer.

"You dare sssumon me, human."

Valentina wiped her eyes, smearing makeup across her face. "Where is Simon? You swore you'd keep him alive. I gave you what you wanted."

The demon's eyes lit with amusement. "He'sss returned to hisss only love. How ssstupid do you feel now?"

She whimpered, but her shoulders straightened. "As long as he's alive, I know he'll come back."

"Sssimon exists in a realm apart from this one. Killed by hisss lover."

"You're lying!"

Valentina lunged forward, but Astaroth dematerialized, and she fell through him, landing on the floor. She let out a cry, pushing up and whirling to face him. "You promised! The price of his life was my soul."

Astaroth tsked. "The pricsse your sssoul paid wasss hisss sssafety from demon kind. I cannot protect him from a naphil."

"You tricked me!" Valentina screamed.

"You ssshould have expected nothing lesss. It'sss time Valentina, for you to make good on your promissse."

Peter tried to shout, to attack Astaroth, but he was helpless to do anything but watch as the demon claimed her soul, leaving her lifeless body to collapse on his bed.

For a few moments, he hovered, taking in the scene, wishing for the hundredth time he had the power to change his past.

When the building shook, debris clouding his view, Peter prayed he'd return to the ether rather than see her body destroyed. Lights flickered. Screams could be heard through the walls. In moments, bits of the ceiling collapsed, objects crashing to the floor as a fissure zigzagged through the middle of his room. His bed, Valentina on it, disappeared into a cloud of darkness.

Without time to guide him, he knew only the insurmountable ache of hopelessness. Despair for all the harm he'd done. The destruction his very existence left in the world. How had he never seen it? His life, afterlife, whatever it was, had been a stain on the world. It was a better place without him in it.

Peter was floating, but something about it felt heavier. It weighed him down, making him feel less insubstantial. He couldn't be sure, but it almost felt like he was moving now. He didn't know where.

But something had changed.

CHAPTER 24

Helena

Helena flexed sore fingers, staring out the window at a blanket of snow that had fallen while she slept. She'd never seen it before, only ever hearing stories from her brother Georgios who sometimes traveled great distances. When she attempted to scoop a handful of the delightful stuff in her hands, it burned, biting into her palms and she'd dropped it, racing back inside to warm her chilled limbs.

Now, she was content to watch it from her place beside the fire.

"Helena?"

"Yes?" she said at the same moment another of the witches did. They glanced at each other and smiled. "Are you called Helena as well?"

The other witch, a woman with long flaxen hair twisted into a single braid down her back, smiled shyly. "I am. You are Aniel's mate, right?"

Helena stood, moving across the room to take a seat beside her. It was becoming easier to understand their strange dialect and she soaked in the words, grateful to have someone to speak with other than Aniel and her brother. "That's right. Are you mated to an angel?"

The other girl laughed. "No. I'm not a Naphil."

Helena's heart sank. She'd hoped at least one other in this coven was like her. She glanced up when the door to the house swung wide and the witch named Vassi strode in. With her shoulders thrust back, and gaze intent, she moved through the room, paying no one any attention. She opened the door to a room in the hall and slammed it.

Helena had seen her twice, but they had yet to meet. She'd planned to introduce herself, but it seemed now wasn't the time. There was something about her. It reminded her of the way Sophia had seemed different from the others. "Is she a Naphil?"

The other Helena smiled. "No. She's like Sophia and me. Changed by Sanura."

Helena's gaze slid over the woman. They were like Lysander. She hadn't noticed it before, but now that she was looking, she saw the way her aura was distorted. It had been bright yellow once. Now it was gray at the edges. The other Helena laced her fingers in her lap and soft white light spilled from them.

"You're a healer!" Helena gasped.

"Call me Hele. It might get confusing if we both go by Helena."

Helena opened her mouth to protest, but the front door banged open and she looked up. She froze as an angel stepped through. She'd seen him once before, chasing Vassi through the fields the day she'd tried and failed to plant carrots. He glared around the room, murder in his eyes, and moved, curling a single wing behind his back.

Another of the witches, one Helena hadn't met yet, stepped forward, but he growled and she shrank away from him.

The room was deadly silent as their gazes tracked his progress. He said nothing, large bare feet tracking dirty footprints as he went. He stopped outside the door Vassi had disappeared into and wrapped his fingers around the knob. It didn't budge, and another rumbling growl erupted from him.

"Vassi. Open the door."

Helena blinked, glancing at the witches watching in rapt silence, clearly unwilling to interfere in whatever was happening.

"What do you want, Michael?" Vassi called through the door.

Michael. The angel Aniel had warned her to avoid. She saw now why he'd advised it. It wasn't the single wing or even the scar running down his back that made him imposing—the naked fury rolling off him was enough to have her preparing to run.

He was silent for a long moment and Helena tensed. Would he turn and end them all in his rage? In truth, she'd seen no one refuse an angel anything before. If the story she'd heard was true, Vassi should have been doubly grateful to him for saving her life.

He grumbled something but released her door handle. His voice was low enough that Helena only heard a single word: *Please.*

She held her breath, waiting for Vassi's next reply. An angel pleading? Unheard of.

The lock sounded, and the door creaked open. Vassi peeked out, gaze taking in their audience, and she opened it wider, grabbing his arm and dragging him into her room. The door slammed again and a collective sigh seemed to be released.

Helena turned back to the witch who asked her to call her Hele, but the front door swung open yet again. She hopped to her feet when Aesop and Zadkiel stepped inside.

"What is it, Brother?" She crossed the space, reaching them in three strides.

"We'd hoped Aniel came here," Aesop said. "Have you spoken with him?"

Helena swallowed a lump rising in her throat. "No. Is there cause for concern?"

"It's Sophia. Something's happened to her."

"What is it? Where is she?" Several women climbed to their feet, clustering around them.

Aesop glanced at the witches crowding closer and backed up a step. Helena drew a deep breath. She should be concerned for the coven's Pythia, but she only felt relief that it wasn't Aniel.

Zadkiel moved, holding up his hands. "Don't worry. We're searching for her now, but we need all the help you can spare. She's somewhere within a fifty-mile radius, but above that, we only know the direction she set out in."

The door behind her opened and Helena spun around as Vassi stepped out, Michael close behind her.

"Brother?" Zadkiel gasped. "It is good to see you."

Michael followed Vassi. Her sisters stepped back, giving him a wide berth as she stopped beside Aesop and his mate.

"I'll go," Vassi offered. "I'm faster and can search the caves and undergrowth. Tell me which direction."

"You will not."

Zadkiel raised a brow at Michael, and Vassi turned, eyeing Michael. "I will, but you're welcome to join me."

"Insufferable," he grumbled.

Vassi searched Michael's face for a long silent moment, then, nodding to herself, turned back. "*We'll* search. Tell us where to go."

Helena bit back her laugh of surprise. The witch gave commands on the scale of a wealthy Eupatridae—not just to a man, but an *angel*. In moments, several other coven members began speaking, offering aid, and Helena shrank from the crowd, eyes widening.

Her coven was close, certainly powerful, but they had never shown such devotion to one of their own. Even their Pythia, who was consulted by prominent men, never inspired such respect. She was forced to consider she may have misjudged Sophia.

"What can I do?" she asked.

Her voice was drowned by the others as they moved quickly, gathering supplies and marching out the door before she could get a word in. Helena stepped aside, trying to keep out of everyone's way.

Soon, the room was empty, and she found herself alone.

CHAPTER 25

Peter

"Please just go." Claire's bright sapphire eyes brimmed with tears. "I don't have long. There's nothing more he can do to me. Run while you still can."

Peter knelt beside her bed, taking her hand in his. They'd had this argument so many times it was hard to say whether this was a stolen memory or simply a memory of Claire before it happened.

He wrapped her fingers in his, squeezing. "I'm not leaving you or the twins."

Her eyelids fluttered closed as she inhaled shallowly.

"Claire? Do you need your inhaler?" Those words had come from Simon. He winced. Claire was the only one of them to need an inhaler and only after some mysterious experiment Alexander performed on her... at seventeen.

He scoured his memory. Did he have any idea what had happened to her? Had that memory of the car accident been erased, or was it new? Had he always used his magic on her? Was she sick because of him in her true past or only in this twisted version of events where his actions somehow affected the past?

Claire didn't answer, lapsing into a fitful sleep.

He stood, releasing her fingers from his grasp, and backed up. If he could change things, could he end Alexander right now and save her from what was coming?

Glancing at her sweat-beaded brow, he frowned. "I'll fix it, Claire."

He raced from the room to Alexander's and yanked the door to the back stairs wide, moving swiftly until he reached the sublevel of the home and stopped outside the metal door. Pressing an ear to it, he listened.

Alexander mumbled to himself.

Peter shoved the door, darting at speed to the place where Alexander's voice came from, and wrapped his fingers around his throat.

Alexander's eyes went wide for a moment before he choked out, "Simon, st..."

Peter squeezed tighter, cutting off the words before Alexander could stop him, and cold satisfaction shot through him as his hold tightened. The room burst into bright orange light as searing pain tore into his arm and he glanced down to see Alexander's flame-tipped fingers wrapped around his forearm, tugging uselessly.

Ignoring the pain, he dug his nails into the side of Alexander's neck, relishing the slick hot blood running over his fingers. His face turned blue, but his gaze flicked left and Peter followed it to the door.

"Release him, Simon." Dianna's bright yellow eyes glinted in the near dark, but Peter's focus wasn't on the night-creature in the doorway.

His grip loosened a fraction as Dianna's sharp nails dug into Claire's too-pale skin, tightening. A thin trickle of blood slid down her arm and Peter released Alexander. The man stumbled backward gasping for air, and bile climbed up Peter's throat.

He knew. He knew where this was going; that it wasn't some heroic gesture he'd only just dreamed up. This was a stolen memory.

This was how Claire became a night-creature.

CHAPTER 26

Michael

"Vassi."

Vassi raced at full speed, intent on leaving Michael behind. But though he couldn't fly, he could still move fast and he gave chase. She darted between massive trunks, sparkling daylight glittering across her skin. Her hair whipped behind her and her scent tugged him along, urging him to follow.

As they ran, a tightness in his chest—one so crushing, it had been centuries since he'd taken a full breath—loosened and the corners of his lips slid up.

She glanced back, her face lit with amusement. She enjoyed seeing his emotions. All of them—the good and the bad. In her room, when he had given in to the fear flooding him, she'd made him grovel. Some wicked part of her seemed to delight, even in that.

Anything but silence, she'd said. *I will accept anything you want to give me but silence.* He rolled the words over, marveling at how freeing they were. She didn't want his kindness or love. She wanted him just as he was.

In an eternity, he had never known how much the judgment weighed on him. Not only from his father, but from his twin, his siblings... and his mate. They had all judged him for being different—the scars he bore, proof of his treachery.

This witch, battered and broken by the traumas of human existence, had no judgement for him. Imperfect as she was, she offered the one thing no one else had: acceptance.

"Keep up, old man." Vassi laughed and ran faster.

"Not a man."

She skidded to a halt, mood going somber, and he stopped beside her, peering down at the thing that had captured her attention. She bent, lifting it gingerly, inspecting it.

"What is it?"

"A walkie-talkie." She bit her lip. "This is how they knew Sophia was within fifty miles. But if it's here, she could be anywhere by now."

A deep furrow marred the skin on her forehead and he was possessed with the urge to rub his thumb over it and smooth her worry away. "She was here. They aren't faster than us. We'll find her."

CHAPTER 27

Peter

Alexander touched his blood-slick throat, eyes narrowing on Peter. "Dianna, bring my daughter."

Dianna dragged Claire on stumbling feet to the center of the room. "Get on the table, Claire."

Claire leaned heavily against the wood, breathing shallowly. "What are you going to do, Alex? I won't survive another of your experiments."

Peter took a step, but Alexander's gaze snapped to him. "Simon. You will not move from that spot until I allow it. You will remain where you are and observe the punishment your actions wrought."

Peter tugged uselessly against Alexander's command. Even with his new name, he was helpless to disobey. "Run, Claire. Get out! He's going to change you."

Something sinister glinted in Alexander's eyes, and his lips stretched into a horrific smile. "How would you know that, I wonder?"

Peter tucked his twitching fingers into his pockets. "You've been trying to prolong her life. It was a guess."

Dianna lifted Claire onto the table and Claire protested only mildly before she collapsed atop it, letting her head fall back. Turning to face Alexander, Dianna said. "I told you. He knows things."

Alexander cocked an eyebrow. "Will it work then? If I kill her?"

Sick dread pooled in Peter's belly. This was wrong. This wasn't how it happened. There had been a demon attack and Claire was dying. Simon had begged Alexander to help her, for anyone to save her. They'd been so close to unlocking Rebecca's memories. He'd been so close to having his love back, his firefly, but she was dying too soon, and he would lose that chance for another two decades.

"Only one way to find out," Dianna said.

Alexander nodded, tugging the worn golden amulet from his pocket. He shot a burst of orange flame at it, sending it spinning.

"Alexander, please. Please don't kill your own daughter."

Alexander glanced over his shoulder as he positioned himself before the table and Claire's weakened form. "You brought this on yourself."

"Please. Use me instead. Take my energy. Don't kill her."

"Simon. Stop talking."

The air expelled from his lungs in a whoosh, and his mouth fell into a flat line. The image blurred as tears welled and he stood silently, watching Alexander thumb through his journal. Claire's eyelids closed and Peter listened to her slow, irregular heartbeat, so much weaker than at twenty-one in any of her other lives. She moaned as she exhaled a soft rattling breath, and agony lanced through him.

He was the cause of her weakened state. The night Zophiel had saved Claire only prolonged the inevitable, but it had given her the time she needed to have Rachael. He knew now that was all she'd cared about. Now, with all the pieces fitted carefully together, he could see the plan had always been to get her to that last life. Zophiel knew what she was doing all along. But one question remained. When had she bound him? It must have been after this life. Otherwise, he wouldn't have been able to do what came next.

Alexander set his book down beside Claire's still form. "Now, my daughter. When this works, Dianna will repeat the spells on me and I will join you in eternity."

Peter fought harder than he ever had, digging deep inside to find the strength to overcome Alexander's spell, but not even his pinky twitched as Alexander pressed both hands to his daughter's chest and cast the spell that drew her last breath.

The spell had taken a great deal from Alexander and he had to rest before the second half could be performed. Dianna remained, watching Claire for any sign Alexander's magic had worked, but Claire was silent and still.

Peter stood motionless, staring at the woman he loved, frozen in death—peaceful—ice coating his veins; he could only wait and watch, praying this time would be different.

Just before dawn, Dianna finally left, saying nothing.

When the single overhead light dimmed, Peter wished his vision would too. Instead, Claire's white nightgown nearly glowed in the windowless room, casting her unmoving chest into stark relief against the dim backdrop and their gargoyle audience.

He longed to go to her, hold her, to whisper prayers for her soul, but none of it would have changed her fate.

When the shift came, he felt it. The moment when he should have gone to Sheol for the day. He expected to find himself in the nothingness he'd floated in between each memory. Instead, the scene transitioned seamlessly to a new night in Alexander's lair. Claire was gone. Did that mean this was a fresh memory? Or merely the next night?

He thought all his prior memories had been leading whatever came next. The path he walked was nearly at its end. Soon, he would reach his destination and discover whether the void he'd jumped into when he left Sheol led to a good end—or bad. Somehow, he was certain whatever the last memory was would determine his fate.

Freed of his compulsion, Peter raced up the stairs, stopping beside the Graves family cemetery to find the fresh mound of dirt beside the place he'd been buried all those years ago.

Alexander had attempted to recreate the events of Simon's death exactly. But Peter knew now that none of Alexander's rituals or spells mattered. Only Sanura had the power to send her back.

Scratching began. It was soft at first, tentative, but in moments it became a desperate, scraping plea. Fear crawled up Peter's throat. For all that had happened in his long afterlife, nothing terrified him quite like the memory of waking inside the coffin that first night.

Glancing around, he spied the shovel used not long before and picked it up, digging as he'd never done before. In minutes, metal struck wood, and he tossed the shovel aside, dropping into the hole and ripping aside a pine plank. Just as with his crudely made coffin, Claire's was a bit of board nailed together—easy to break out of.

A hand shot through the hole, clawing its way up. A second hand wrapped around broken wood and it cracked under her new strength, falling away to reveal a dirt-streaked Claire, wild-eyed with terror.

Peter leaned down, holding out a hand, and she took it, nearly yanking him in with her new strength. He wedged his feet against the side of the boards and hefted her out. She sprang free, leaping from the hole, and landing gracefully on loose dirt.

Peter followed her out and brushed off his knees. "Claire."

Her bright yellow gaze shot to him, but her eyes were unfocused, feral, just as he'd remembered. The bit of hope he'd clung to died when the beast Claire had become eyed him coldly.

A door banged shut on the fourth floor of the Graves mansion and Claire's head darted left preternaturally fast. She dug her heel into the ground and dashed toward the sound.

"Claire, wait!"

Peter chased her through the back door, up the stairs, and past Alexander's room to Rhea's. A soft sniffle was shushed as Rhea hummed softly and Peter stopped outside the door to her room.

"Claire. You can't hurt them. They're your babies," he whispered.

Claire crouched low, poised like a cat to spring. She darted into the room, but Peter was faster, tackling her to the floor and rolling with her into a corner.

Rhea looked up and Rachel burst into a wailing cry as he wrestled Claire into submission.

Her bright yellow eyes were trained on Rhea, a baby in her arms, and Peter would never know which was her intended target. Her arms bent, nearly overpowering him. She was stronger, and a lifetime of what could have been flashed through his mind as canines lengthened along his lips.

He struck.

He sucked, pulling out the lingering in Claire's veins, taking with it any essence that remained. Her strength waned. It was enough to stop her for now—his rational mind knew it—but something drove him to keep going.

Some involuntary push to end her once and for all.

He sucked and sucked even as it became hard to pull anything from her unmoving form. Even as the blood cooled and coagulated on his tongue, he continued.

CHAPTER 28

Sophia

Sophia tripped over a rock, swearing as her knee struck the sharp object. Cassia yanked hard on the chain binding her and she slid several inches before getting her feet under her and running to catch up.

"I'm not as fast as you," Sophia seethed as she tripped again, pain radiating from her sore knee.

Cassia said nothing, continuing to drag her along. They'd moved at this breakneck speed for hours and Sophia had given up cataloging the aches accompanying them on their trek. She'd never realized how fast Cassia was compared with the rest of them. Though she'd seen Simon move like something out of a nightmare, rivaling the angels themselves, none of her other sisters scratched the surface of that kind of speed. None, it seemed, except Cassia.

She wondered if it had something to do with her dominant gift of fire or some sort of gift in exchange for the deal she'd made with Sanura. Could speed be gifted? If so, Sophia was certain Sanura would have been the one to know how to do it.

When the moon was high, they stopped. And though they'd come down from Cassia's mountain hideout, the wind whipped at Sophia's skin, sending sparks of icy cold down her back. Her teeth chattered, and she swore to herself that she'd never leave a coat behind again if she survived this.

Once, the cold hadn't affected her. She'd formed a protective barrier around herself that kept the elements at bay. How she longed to return to that time—when the Earth was a place for living things. Not that she'd been counted among them for some time.

Cassia wrapped her chains tightly around her arm and glanced over her shoulder at Sophia. She pursed her lips, and her brow dipped. "Make a sound and I gut you where you stand. I'll leave your body for the humans to clean up."

Sophia stiffened, forcing her trembling limbs to still. This Cassia wasn't the girl she'd grown up with, the one she'd learned to say her first words beside or cast spells with behind Yia-Yia's back when they were supposed to be studying math. Who was this cold, heartless creature?

Cassia searched her face for any sign of defiance. Seeing none, she gave Sophia's chains another yank and pulled her behind the cliff wall just outside the bunker General Vaughn and his men had taken shelter in when the angels and demons destroyed the planet.

The door to the massive vault had remained open since the day Leah and Gabriel appeared and led them all out into the light. The day Sophia had seen the sun for the first time since her death. She hadn't thought beyond surviving the elements when she concocted this plan, but now that she was here, she'd have to do better if she hoped to survive the night.

"He's in the general's old living quarters. It was the only room he couldn't break out of." Sophia's soft words carried on a chill breeze and Cassia nodded, not looking back.

They remained pressed against the sheer rock wall for an eternity as Cassia's gaze flicked nervously back and forth. Her paranoia was bordering on manic. No one had come or gone since they'd stopped here, and there were no signs anyone would. This late at night, everyone at camp would be sleeping. They had little to fear these days, or so they thought. Sophia hoped their blissful ignorance wouldn't be their end.

Cassia darted out from their hiding place, moving at a dizzying speed. Sophia had to work hard not to be dragged. By the way Cassia moved, she was certain she would have hauled her mangled body over rough terrain to ensure no one saw, regardless of the cost to Sophia.

When they reached the door to the bunker, Cassia towed Sophia behind her and turned, wedging her shoulder into the massive steel door.

Sophia's heart climbed into her throat. If they were trapped inside, there would be no escape for her. "Wait!" She backed up, pulling hard on her chains. "If you close the door, it will lock. We don't have the code."

Cassia ignored Sophia's protests, shoving with all her might. Slowly, it was inching together, the silver light of the moon sliding menacingly across the floor. Sophia felt in her bones that if it closed, her chance for escape would be sealed on the other side. "We'll be trapped until morning and when the general arrives to find the door closed, he'll know we're in here."

Cassia paused, spinning around. "You think I can't take a few puny humans?"

"They have weapons. Enough to take down the demons. No one is invincible, Cassia. Now that Heaven and Hell no longer exist, this is it. You die here, it's forever."

Cassia eyed her, saying nothing, then pushed off the door, dragging Sophia with her.

"It's straight back, through the soldier's barracks. I'll show you the way."

"No need. I've been here many times."

Fear tightened like a collar around Sophia's throat. Cassia knew her way around and Sophia had just given Peter's supposed location. What was stopping Cassia from killing her now? Goosebumps erupted along her frozen arms. Hours in chains, being towed along over rough terrain in freezing cold conditions, had nearly numbed every part of her, but the realization that she'd given away her hand without even knowing it was a shock to her senses.

Think Sophia. When they discovered Peter wasn't there, she'd have to come up with some alternate location they might have taken him, somewhere that would lead them on a goose chase through the night. If she was lucky, an angel would cross their path, but she wouldn't rely on that hope alone.

"Sister?" a voice near the entrance called into the cavernous space. His strange ancient accent could only make him Helena's brother. Mate of Zadkiel.

In a blur, Cassia was behind Sophia, arm wrapped around her neck, hand over her mouth. Sophia's heart beat against the arm, squeezing her oxygen supply. *Run*, her mind screamed, but Cassia wouldn't let her get away. If she bit down on the hand, muffling her sound—screamed for help—would the Naphil reach her before Cassia had drained her dry?

"Sister? I saw someone come in here. This is no time for jokes. Everyone's looking for you. We're worried."

Something flashed in Sophia's periphery and searing heat scorched her cheek as flaming hands wrapped around Cassia's arm, wrenching her away. Sophia spun around, mouth falling slack as Helena wrestled Cassia to the ground, limbs alight with flame.

Sophia was frozen in place, watching the scene in utter confusion for a moment before Aesop appeared beside her and joined the fight. His fire was blue, like Leah's, and she knew this must be her direct ancestor. The pair of Nephilim had Cassia pinned down, and she was a ball of red flames, but they were immune to her magic. Sophia said a quick prayer the siblings were strong enough to subdue her.

Cassia brought her knee up in a blur.

"Lookout!"

Sophia winced as her cousin's knee hit its mark. Aesop doubled over. She reared back, swinging her head into Helena's. Dazed, Helena's hold loosened on Cassia's shoulders.

She slammed her head into the Naphil's again and Helena dropped to the ground. Sophia backed up, powerless in her chains, and Cassia stalked toward her. "You tricked me! I'll kill you!" Cassia lurched forward, but she was caught in midair as time froze.

Sophia tried to turn her head to see who'd entered, but it was like swimming through molasses. Twice, she'd been caught in a time bubble, but both times, she'd been unable to move. Even her eyes were stuck in their position.

"My dove." Aniel darted past Sophia as she stood frozen, watching him collide with Helena. He lifted her to her feet, turning her head left and right, kissing her cheeks, her forehead, her hands. She threw her arms around her angel and they stayed that way for a small eternity.

Something in Sophia's chest fractured at the sight. She was not destined for great love. She wasn't destined for *any* love. She would live out this miserable eternity alone or die and disappear into the black nothingness of oblivion.

Aesop groaned on the floor and Aniel released Helena, stooping to help him up. He dusted off his pants, before they all turned their attention to Cassia.

Aesop moved closer to her. "There is something wrong with her aura. Sister, can you see it? "

Helena squinted. "I see nothing. But better safe than sorry. Let's kill her." Helena looked at both men for confirmation. Aniel gave a quick shake of his head and Aesop frowned.

"Sister, we cannot pass judgment. Ours is not the place to end a life. Even one such as hers."

"We've ended the demons," Aniel said. "And my dove is right. I do sense something strange with her soul. Not a demon—but..."

Helena nodded, resting a hand on Aniel's arm. "My mate speaks true. She would have become a demon if the world had not ended."

Sophia reached for her gifts, begged them to grant her this gift of speech. She would speak for her sister. Be the voice she needed when none had been before. Cassia only wanted to be treated as an equal. But here stood three creatures who would judge her without knowing her. She pressed against the confines of time, but couldn't move.

Internally, she gave a frustrated scream. When Dina spoke with Rebecca, Sophia hadn't tried to move; it had not seemed right to interfere in the affairs of angels then. Now she knew better. They were imperfect beings, capable of making mistakes. And they were about to make one now.

She pushed the bounds of her water magic, searching the time spell weaving the elements together. There—a thread. If she could only pull it.

"What is the meaning of this?"

The scraping, gravely voice of the one-winged angel would have frozen Sophia if she weren't already bound by magic. He stepped past her, giving her a perfect view of his back, and Sophia stared at the angry scar down his left shoulder blade. Instead of a white line or even a red mark, shimmering gold traced the path over his skin, marking the place a matching wing once bloomed from flesh.

He was the only one winged angel she'd ever seen. What had he done to deserve such a fate? Why, when Gabriel had regrown an entire head, had this angel not recovered?

"We are debating the fate of this Nasdaqu-ush, Michael." Aniel left Helena's side, moving to block her view of the deformed creature.

Michael circled Cassia, inspecting her every scar and flaw. "What has she done?"

"Captured this witch. And she stole food."

Michael eyed Helena as if he wasn't used to being spoken to so directly or with so much insolence. He returned his gaze to Cassia, continuing to circle her.

"Human affairs. Not our concern or our business to punish."

"This is the creature who attacked Vassi, Brother." Zadkiel took a step back when Michael's menacing glare flashed to him. There was enough malice in his eyes that Sophia knew Zadkiel had just signed Cassia's death warrant with those words.

In desperation, she funneled her energy into her strongest gift, pushing with all her might against the magic in her bonds and the air. She had to stop him. Cassia would have killed her, she was sure, but even knowing that truth, Sophia couldn't stand by and watch her sister die.

Her lips twitched, the cords in her neck flexing. She pushed harder.

Michael had stopped circling. Now he was face to face with Cassia. "I want to look upon the creature who dared harm my..." He trailed off, glancing around the room. "Companion." He raised a hand.

Sophia pulled with everything she had at the energy thrumming inside her and a cry burst from her lips. "No!"

All eyes swiveled to her. Michael's hand fell, and he stalked toward her. She would have shrunk from the black fury in his eyes, but she had used every drop of magic at her disposal and was helpless to do more than watch as he approached.

CHAPTER 29

Peter

Peter gasped, stumbling forward. Claire caught him.

"Simon. Are you well?"

Not Claire. Sarah. The awful memory of the night he'd killed his love was so fresh he tasted her blood on his tongue, felt her stiff, cooling flesh in his arms. She'd been right there, alive and warm, and he had taken too much. Why? It hardly mattered. There was no coming back from that.

A sob escaped him, and he sank to the ground. Whatever this new horror was, he didn't have it in him to go on. He couldn't endure any more.

Sarah dropped to her knees beside him, wrapping an arm around his shoulders. "What is it, my love?"

"I'm so sorry." He covered his face with his hands, unable to look at her, to see the best version of them. Her words came back to him. *My love. My love!* He looked up. "Rebecca?"

Her brow furrowed. "Who else?"

Peter swiveled, throwing his arms around her and tackling her to the ground. He peppered her face and neck with kisses, ignoring her protests. Given the size of the trees in the orchard, it must be the time after Rebecca regained her memories in Sarah's life. When they'd had nearly two years together. His fondest memories were from this uncomplicated time in their lives; when the magic of Rebecca's gifted second life seemed like a blessing and they had yet to learn of the curse. Before Claire's death, Rachel and Robert's disappearance, Valentina or any of the other mistakes that would ultimately be their ruin.

He lifted himself, searching her face. Her dark lashes blinked open, and she stared back. The smile on her pink lips faltered, and she slid out from under him. "What is it, Simon? Something's wrong. Tell me."

He shook his head, having no idea how long he would have with her. A moment? A night? Would he close his eyes and wake in the void or in some new, terrible memory of his worst mistakes? "Nothing. I missed you."

She laughed, lifting and pressing a soft kiss to his lips. "I'm right here."

He sank onto his elbows, caging her in and letting his mouth hover just over hers. Her warm breath mingled with his and the horror of his last memory bled away. He would trade his soul for an eternity in this part of his past. To be trapped here forever. "I never want to leave you."

"Then don't."

His mouth found hers, sucking her lower lip as he slid his tongue in, tasting the sweetness and letting it erase the blood he still felt coating it. He was lost in the moment, in her, and a small eternity passed before the pair came up for air.

He sat up, leaning against the old oak tree, and tugged her with him to rest against his chest. They sat in silence, listening to the crickets. Her heart rate slowed, her breathing becoming deeper, and he leaned his nose against her head, inhaling her scent.

Light appeared in the orchard. Peter held up a hand shielding his eyes. Atop him, Rebecca remained still as Zophiel landed beside them, her glow dimming until she might have almost passed for human.

"What do you want?" he hissed.

She stopped, eyeing him warily. "This must be your future self. You don't seem at all surprised to see me."

"Yes. And future me knows you've ruined Rebecca's life." A streak of lightning shot across the sky, illuminating the angel's harsh stare. Ethereal as she was, Peter saw only a villain when he looked at her now. He shifted under Rebecca's weight, wrapping an arm protectively around her. "Leave us alone. We want nothing from you."

Zophiel surprised him by dropping to a knee beside them. His grip tightened on Rebecca and he leaned back, putting what little space between them he could without waking her.

"Ah, but you forget. My kind were not made to serve you. We serve the greater good, no matter the cost to human life. And now, it's your turn to serve."

A bolt of terror shot through Peter. Her words were cold, alien. A reminder that she held none of his human emotions. No heart beat in that chest. Had she ever cared for any of them? He tensed, preparing to wake Rebecca and escape the mad creature, but the air stilled, the hairs on the back of his neck rising. A soft glow illuminated the edges of the angel crouched beside him.

He remembered none of this. *Another memory stolen.*

"Simon Carey, I bind you. From this day until my last, you exist for one purpose."

He tried to open his mouth, to protest her words, but he was frozen, helpless, as he had been so many times in his long life.

"You exist to ensure Rebecca's line continues. Nothing matters but her safety. You will kill for her."

His heart picked up speed, and a trickle of sweat ran down his back. "Die for her."

His throat was dry as she continued.

"Protect her against any foe. Herself included."

His vision tunneled, narrowing on a spec of light before him as the magic of her words coated his skin, sinking in.

"If she dies, you die. The day she draws final breath, so too shall you."

Zophiel disappeared in a blink.

Peter gasped as the last words pierced his heart. His mind raced at the implications of that binding, and suddenly he understood. The times she'd died in all her previous lives, the magic didn't care, so long as a child lived to carry her soul. It wasn't until Allie's life that he'd felt he was dying too.

Every near-death moment became clear: Claire's accident before the children, Allie at seventeen and Rebecca on Grace Island. Claire's attack on her children... None of those times had been his fault. He was bound. Rebecca had had no part in it.

Zophiel was the sole architect of his tortured existence.

"Rebecca." He shook her.

She stirred in his arms and some of the ice chilling his veins un-thawed. Was it a mercy to know the truth when it was too late to change it? When he would leave this memory and return to the consequences of his actions?

"Rebecca. Wake up."

She mumbled, turning to her side and curling an arm around him. He exhaled a ragged breath, reveling for a moment in her comforting touch. Whatever waited for him, he would never have this again. Why race toward the empty nothing that was coming for him?

Settling against the tree, he loosened his hold on her, closing his eyes and listening to the steady beat of her heart. In this life, she'd been healthy nearly till the end. They'd had more than a year of bliss. If he could bottle this moment and keep it, he would stay here forever.

Peter woke, the absence of Rebecca's warmth, a bucket of ice against his skin. He shot up, taking in his new surroundings. After over six months in the memory with Rebecca, he'd grown used to their life. Those first few weeks, every time he closed his eyes, he expected to end up in the void. Instead, no time passed. It was night and when he opened his eyes; it was the next evening. He never went to Sheol or a different memory.

After so many months, he'd let his guard down, daring to believe it might be his eternity after all. It hadn't been perfect. Alexander called on him to do his bidding and Rebecca's temper flared often, but he swallowed it all gratefully.

But his new surroundings were something out of a nightmare: a dystopian reality where Earth was a charred remnant of the one he had left so many months ago. Had it been months? Was he even truly here? He ran a hand down his chest, the same fabric he'd worn in Sheol soft against his fingers.

This was the first time he'd woken to such clear detail. It was a world he didn't recognize and all his senses were alive. In most of his memories, something was missing: smell, feeling, the ability to control his actions. Here, he felt it all. With a sinking sensation, he spun around, the long journey, spanning some indefinite period was finally at its end.

He'd arrived on the mortal plane.

A sign hung half haphazardly against what remained of a brick building. He could make out a few words: ***Blackbeard's Ta***. He didn't need to see the rest to know it was all that was left of one of the three restaurants that had existed in Bath, North Carolina. Truly, it was the only way to tell where he was. On three sides, jagged fissures zig-zagged along blackened earth and far below, red liquid filled with debris—and what looked like bodies-raced toward the ocean.

He spun in a slow circle, orienting himself to this new Earth, and stopped when he faced inland. As far as the eye could see, fires sent plumes of smoke into the sky and nothing living remained—nothing here, at least.

After days moving over uneven terrain and through mostly destroyed forest, a shadow swept overhead. Peter ducked under a fallen tree and peered up. A pair of massive wings swept by, flapping several times and gliding away. Angels were here. Not a good sign for him, but wherever the angel was headed, people may be.

CHAPTER 30

Helena

"Michael, stop!" Helena's nails dug into Aniel's arm. "Aniel, stop him!" Sophia did not deserve to die, especially not at the hands of the angel with a screw loose. Where was the witch who knew how to control him? She was the only one he'd listen to.

"Brother, it is not a crime to defy our magic." Aniel held his hands up. "Leave the witch."

"She's no witch. She's a Nasdaqu-ush."

"Where's Vassi, Brother? Were you not with her tonight?" Aniel lowered his hands, wrapping them around Helena's.

"She's caught in your obnoxiously large time bubble." Michael rolled his eyes and Helena gaped. Maybe he wasn't in a murderous mood. Perhaps his face just looked that way.

"Is it wise to leave her outside alone, Michael?" Aesop's first words since Michael's arrival startled Helena and her gaze swung to her brother. He turned to Aniel. "Release time and let us speak to the creature. Bring Vassi in as well."

"Wait." Zadkiel stepped forward, raising his hands with a flourish, and released Sophia's bonds. "Let us use these." He snapped them shut over Cassia's frozen wrists.

"That was unwise," Michael grumbled. "This creature clearly has more angelic blood than most. Look how she fights our time restraints even now."

"She is not a danger to us." Helena squeezed Aniel's hand, searching his face. He nodded, releasing his time bubble.

Sophia stumbled forward, throwing her arms around Cassia. Cassia startled, gazed down at her wrists, then at Sophia. She hissed, wriggling in her bonds, but it was no use. Only the angels could release her now. Whatever Zadkiel had done to them, they were not bound by Cassia's magic any longer.

The air shifted as Michael turned and Vassi raced into the room. She hovered several feet away, eyeing the group warily. Michael beckoned her forward. Zadkiel and Aniel gasped in unison.

Helena didn't know the angel, but it was clear the others feared him.

"Vassi. Look upon your attacker as I end her."

Helena blanched. She understood why they were concerned. He was a murderous creature.

"No." It was a single word, falling softly from Vassi's lips, but the air seemed to freeze as Michael turned, giving the room his back.

Sophia continued to squeeze Cassia tightly; she looked like she would roast her alive if she had access to her magic.

"No?!" Michael folded his arms over his chest. "Do you not want retribution for your injury?"

"No." Vassi mimicked Michael's pose, gripping her biceps tightly. "My sister does not deserve death at your hands. No one does."

The anger radiating off Michael simmered between them and he stood, staring Vassi down. She stared back, raising a brow.

The silent tension was disrupted by the sound of flapping wings. In moments, the massive steel door was shoved wide and Raphael strode in, the outline of a man—silhouetted in shadow—following close behind.

All eyes swiveled to the pair, and Cassia whispered. "Peter?"

Helena glanced at Cassia, nose scrunching as she puzzled out the name. She'd heard it before, but couldn't remember where. Was he the person who had disappeared? The one the others were out searching for? He didn't look like much for all the fuss. He was handsome enough, nothing to her angel, with his fiery curls and matching eyes.

I'll take that compliment, my dove.

Helena flashed a smile at her mate.

A scream rent the air, and Helena's gaze darted toward the sound as everything seemed to move in slow motion.

Cassia's eyes brightened to liquid gold, her nails lengthening as her bonds snapped in half. She dragged sharp points up Sophia's arms. Sophia's cry was deafening. She fell back just as Vassi raced forward, shoving Cassia to the ground.

Cassia was on her feet too fast, moving in a blur and she punched Vassi's chest, nails digging into flesh. Vassi dropped to her knees, face going pale, something like shock registering in her expression.

Cassia turned, a wicked gleam in her eye as she faced the room. She let the object in her hands drop to the floor and Helena's mouth parted as Cassia held her fingers to her mouth, licking crimson-covered tips.

Zadkiel and Michael reached her at the same time, but she backed up, blurring into the darkness faster than either of them. Michael fell to his knees beside Vassi. His hands came up, catching her as her eyes closed and he settled her head into his lap. He bent close to her mouth, listening for signs of breathing, but she must be dead. No one could live without a heart.

Michael was oblivious to everyone watching as he pressed his lips to hers in a chaste kiss. He lifted his hands, a soft white light flaring to life under his palms as he pressed them over the gaping wound in her chest.

Helena was no healer, but she was certain even an angel couldn't heal an injury that severe. She glanced away as Michael pressed his lips to Vassi's again, feeling she was intruding on a private moment.

She looked left as feathers dusted her nose—Zadkiel and her mate giving chase. Her heart thrummed in her chest. If the night creature would tear a heart out, there was no telling what she would do to the angels if cornered. *Don't go, my love!*

We must stop her, Dove. Stay here. I will return soon.

Her heart lurched in her chest as he raced away with Aesop's mate.

"There's no way out," Zadkiel called.

Aniel nodded, and the pair disappeared into the darkness.

Peter dropped beside Michael and Vassi. "I can help."

Michael lifted his lip, snarling at him. "Touch her and you lose a hand."

Helena had forgotten Peter was there. He'd been silent until now.

Sophia sank to her knees beside them and whispered in Peter's ear. They clearly knew one another. Helena heard her say something about an amulet, and at that Peter stuck his hand in his pocket and held out an empty palm. The color drained from his face as Aesop joined them on the floor.

Only Helena and Raphael stood back as the one-winged angel's hands glowed brightly. A trail of red ran along the dirt floor, but each second the angel held his glowing hands over Vassi's wound, it slowed; soon, it was nothing but a stain on the floor. Helena gasped when he bit into his arm, tearing a gash in it.

"Brother, you can't," Raphael hissed.

Michael's eyes narrowed to slits. "Can't I?"

"She's not your analogous umbra."

Michael tipped his arm to Vassi's mouth, and golden blood spilled onto her lips. "It's my part of our soul and I'll share it with whom I choose."

"But Mary—"

The violence in Michael's eyes was enough to cut steel. Raphael closed his mouth. Helena watched in wonder as he dropped to his knees beside his twin, tearing open his own wrist. Michael growled low in his throat, but didn't stop Raphael from letting the blood fall into Vassi's mouth.

Sophia stopped whispering, squeezing Peter's arm tightly when Vassi's eyes flew open and she sucked in a great heaving breath. Aesop jumped to his feet, rushing to Helena's side. "It's a miracle, is it not, sister?"

"Yes," Helena breathed, mouth hanging open as Michael helped the witch to her feet.

Sophia hopped up, throwing her arms around Vassi, and pushing Michael aside. He stared daggers at the back of Sophia's head, but said nothing. Slowly, she backed up, revealing the witch who had just been brought back to life. Beside her, on the dusty floor, the lifeless organ she no longer needed lay forgotten.

Michael held out a hand, and Vassi wrapped her tanned fingers around them. Her gaze was dazed, but in moments her vision cleared, landing on Michael. "That's twice you've saved me." Her voice was scratchy, faint white lines trailing across her throat.

For a long moment, Vassi and her broken angel stared at one another. Helena could have sworn they were having a silent conversation, the kind she had Aniel often had. Michael broke their stare. "What did you say Nasdaqu-ush?"

Sophia and Peter stopped their hushed conversation, glancing to the angel. "She has the amulet."

Michael's gaze shot to Raphael. "Brother. Come with me." To Sophia, he said. "Can you protect your sister for even a moment? I realize I am asking a great deal."

Sophia's brows lowered, and Helena almost laughed as her hand landed on her hip. "I protect my coven every day. You don't get to swoop in here in the most dire of moments, act like a hero, then tell me I'm worthless."

Michael's lip curled back, but Raphael wrapped an arm around his biceps, tugging him away. "Come, Michael."

Michael shot another glance at Vassi, and she nodded. "Go. I'll be here when you return."

The pair of angels who truly embodied the word with their cherubic curls, white wings and tanned skin disappeared, leaving the witches alone.

CHAPTER 31

Michael

Michael raced into the dark, chasing the scent of the Nasdaqu-ush who was mother to all her creatures. "We must stop her. Only we can."

Raphael glanced at him, a grimace on his face. "Would you truly end her, Brother?"

"My reticence to act has caused all this. I see that now."

"No one blames you—"

"You all do!"

Michael stopped beside a pile of ammunition boxes. Had he not been so distracted by the witch, he would have noticed the faint traces of her scent earlier. *His* scent. She'd stolen the witch's body, using it to continue her crusade. What she hoped to accomplish now, he could not say.

Perhaps her true mission was revenge against the one who stole her mate from her—punishment no child deserved. But the power she would have given his fallen brother would have been catastrophic. And she had proven time and again that any goodness once residing in her was swallowed by the darkness corroding her soul. He wished he could relieve her of the tainted gift, but he hadn't known what her birth would mean.

He had yet to find his soulmate when he met the lovely Shalim. She was fetching water when he found her. In that time, all seraphim roamed the Earth, desperate to find their other half, to restore what was lost to them. Her soft melody called to him on a faint breeze, drawing him like a mirage in the desert. Greedily, he drank, and after they'd lain together, his soul still fractured, she confessed she would marry a human man within the week.

"Hi Dad."

Michael spun around.

She didn't have Sanura's face, but her golden eyes—the color of his blood—and that vicious smile, could only belong to his daughter.

"There is no place for you here, Sanura."

Her smile dropped just as Raphael slid to a stop beside him. "Uncle." Her gaze swiveled between them, landing on Michael. "How does it feel knowing you carry that scar for your ill-begotten mistake?"

"You're no mistake. Your actions were."

Sanura scoffed. "I never had a choice. Your tainted magic made me what I am. Letting my mate think his fallen status was the reason for my magic was a cruel joke, but giving me a gift the world feared was worse."

Michael's chest ached at the truth in her words. Why, of all the seraphim, had he been given the power to raise the dead? Had this twisted gift manifested from some darkness within him?

When Sanura was born, Michael was knee-deep in demon blood, cleaning up another fallen city. A blow which should have healed quickly sent him to his knees and when he rose, his wing was gone. He waited hours for it to heal, then a day. Finally, Raphael helped him return to Alaxia. There, he prayed it would heal, but while all the others came and went, healed from their every wound, he remained fragmented.

For a decade, he traced and retraced his every action, seeking the answer to his punishment. He would not learn of her birth until she was a woman, and Gabriel received his new mission.

"I had no hand in that deception, but I am eternally sorry, Daughter."

"I don't want your pity. I want blood—yours and Gabriel's for ending my mate," she said. "You both played a part in it. Or perhaps I should take your mates and let you spend the rest of eternity as I will: alone."

"No," Raphael shouted.

The ache was a knife that twisted painfully in Michael's chest. He knew what it meant to be alone. It had been his companion these many millennia. "Revenge does not heal a broken heart, Daughter."

Movement at the edge of Michael's vision caught his eye, and he glanced left. Sanura darted toward the darkness, but he threw up his hands, calling the death surrounding them. Dead wood and metal bent by human hands unfolded at his command, reforming around her.

Screaming, she scraped violently at her cage. She fought, setting burning hands on the wood. It crackled and spit, but under his control the particles held and bits of metal pushed in, forming an impenetrable wall. Her gift rose, pushing the bounds of her cage, but her power had never held a candle to his. Her attempts were futile.

"Brother, the moment is now." Aniel appeared beside him, resting a hand on his shoulder.

He shrugged out of his touch, a shudder rolling through him. Zadkiel appeared beside him, and the group stood around Sanura's makeshift cage. "I know the sacrifice we're asking," Zadkiel said. "But she must be stopped."

Bitterness rose in Michael. They were right back where it started, three thousand years ago. Before any of them had found their soulmate. Except Aniel. Sanura had destroyed a city, wiping out a third of

Dina's line and sending several soulmates to Alaxia before they'd ever crossed paths with their seraph on the mortal plane.

She must be stopped once and for all, and only he could do it.

"This time would be final," he breathed. More to himself than the others.

Aniel's gaze darkened. "She will kill more humans. She has attempted to kill your new friend twice."

Sanura froze, eyebrow raising, and the power thrumming through Michael sped up. She would use that information. Perhaps she already had. Was it the true reason she'd attacked Vassi? "Do you seek your end, Sanura?"

She studied him for some time, and his siblings said nothing, knowing the decision was his alone. Her gaze shot past him and he turned to see three Nasdaqu-ush moving through the dark. They stopped beside the group. Sophia, Vassi and the man Sanura had been searching for.

"Do it," Sanura said, drawing his attention back to her.

It was an intentional misdirection, and his gaze swiveled back to Peter. His soul still lived inside him, but there was a faint signature, one Michael recognized. He tilted his head, stepping closer and inhaling deeply. "My daughter has been busy," he said, stepping back.

Her brows lowered and though her features were that of the witch whose body she inhabited, the expression was all Sanura.

"Is there enough of your soul in him to remain if I end you?"

Her lips fell into a flat line, and her gaze trailed over the group before returning to him. "Enough to influence his decisions. Would that clear your conscience? Wipe away any remorse for killing your only daughter if you end this vessel?"

Michael tsked. "Come now Sanura, you know I control everything dead. It would be but a snap of my fingers to remove all traces of you from this plane."

Sanura backed up in her cage. "You wouldn't."

A hand landed on Michael's shoulder and he twitched to remove it, but something in him strained toward her touch; he was reminded again of what it felt like to be near one's soulmate. It was stronger now that he and Raphael had fed part of their soul to revive her. Perhaps she could be called such a thing now, with so much of their soul living in her. Fleetingly, he wondered if he could find solace with the witch beside him.

Show her mercy, Stranger.

His lips twitched. It shouldn't have been possible, but somehow, when Vassi touched him, she could speak into his mind. It was new. Something that began after she died and was brought back to life—a mockery of what his siblings had—but he found he liked it. Craved it. Wanted to hear her voice inside his mind always.

You would get tired of that, she replied.

Never.

Vassi's lips split in a wide grin. *Well then, Stranger, would you like a story?*

"Brother, could we not remove her gift? As we did with Samael?" Raphael's voice startled him from their inner dialogue and he glanced at his twin. Could they? Was it as simple as that?

"No!" Sanura shouted. "You can't. I need my gift. It's all I have now that he's gone." Her voice cracked, spearing pain through Michael's chest.

"You'll need to end us both." Peter stepped forward, meeting each of their eyes.

CHAPTER 32

Peter

Peter's mind was a roiling turmoil of contradictions. He'd believed every truth had been revealed in the void when memory after memory uncovered more missing moments from his life. But this new truth was more than he could bear. A piece of Sanura had lived in him all these years, influencing his decisions—a leech, surviving off him.

She could never truly be killed until he was. He'd lived a long tortured existence, thinking he'd always been alone. But she was there through all of it. Protecting the part of her soul she knew guaranteed her safety.

He had been a pawn—he and Rebecca both had—in some bigger game, but unlike Rebecca, he had always been on the wrong side. While she existed to complete Gabriel, an angel tasked with ending the devil, Simon's sole purpose had been to ensure Sanura would never die.

He understood now why he'd been given those six months of relative peace. It made the knowledge more bearable. True death, a death with no promise of eternity, was terrifying, but Peter had seen what came after, and he'd already had his happy ending. He would do this thing to ensure the rest of them could live in peace.

"Do it. End us. It's the only way to be sure."

The angel, whose face lived in a permanent scowl unless he was looking at Vassi, frowned, and there was genuine anguish in his eyes. Vassi's hand slid down his arm, fingers lacing in the angel's. They stared at one another, some silent conversation playing out. It reminded Peter of Rebecca and Gabriel. The way they seemed to forget anyone existed but the two of them.

He cleared his throat, but Raphael shook his head.

Cassia—or Sanura—tapped her nails against the cage Michael had trapped her in. It was a marvel of magical ability and one he had seen no other of their kind wield. Peter was beginning to believe he had no idea what the angels were capable of.

Michael nodded, turning to his twin. "We will strip them of their magic and give them the opportunity to join the community. If they fail, I'll end them myself."

Sophia stirred from whatever thoughts she'd been trapped in. "Will you take her speed?"

"Yes." Michael released Vassi's hand, moving to stand beside his brother. "Let us remove the man's gifts first, to ensure she has nowhere to escape."

Sanura screamed at Michael, flinging insults, cursing him, and spitting on the ground. He ignored her, motioning to Peter, who moved numbly. He'd been human again not so long ago. It was miserable, but then, the drive to protect Rebecca nearly had him crawling out of his skin. Now, with no compulsion and the promise of freedom from Sanura, he walked on steady legs.

Michael and Raphael surrounded him, linking hands.

"Wait!" Sophia ducked under them and threw her arms around Peter. She pressed her nose to his neck, squeezing tight. "No matter what, you'll have a place with us."

He hugged her back and exhaled a shaky breath. He hadn't known how much he needed that reassurance—confirmation that he would fit somewhere when he had nothing left to offer—until she gave it.

Sophia released him, stepped out of the circle, and nodded to Peter as he closed his eyes. He sucked in a sharp breath, letting his mind drift back to his last night with Rebecca. They'd been in their favorite spot, under the oak tree beside the orchard, staring up at the glittering stars. She'd told him she loved him for the hundredth time, but it never got old.

In the memory, a place that never existed for anyone but him, he had told her the truth about Zophiel, the binding that meant he would keep her safe and lever leave her side. He told her of the future and all that would come, leaving out the parts about Gabriel. She'd cried and said she didn't want to die, but in that version of reality, Rebecca had accepted it. He told her how she died in Claire's life and kissing his tear-stained cheeks, she had forgiven him.

It was better than he deserved, proof that it was only a dream.

When he opened his eyes again, he held out a hand. It was blurry and out of focus. He glanced around at the darkened room, at the shapes surrounding him. "I think I need glasses."

Sophia laughed, appearing by his side too fast for him to track, and wrapped an arm around him. "Come on old man, I know someone who can fix you up."

"Old? Am I wrinkled?" He reached up, running a hand over his face and letting out a sigh. "You're not funny." Sophia chuckled, leading him out. "Shouldn't we stay to see what happens to Sanura?"

"She has enough witnesses." Sophia bumped his side.

They left the bunker, following the road lit only by moonlight at a glacial pace. The chill air whipped at Peter's neck and back, sending goosebumps rippling down his arms. They reached a suburb with rows of nearly identical homes lining intersecting streets.

Peter would have asked why they'd chosen this small suburban neighborhood to settle in had he not seen firsthand how little of the world remained as Raphael carried him here. It might be the last place standing on Earth.

Sophia stopped at a home with tan shutters and a red door and pushed it open. Inside, all was silent and still. Peter collapsed into a chair, his feet aching after the long walk. He groaned, kicking his shoes off and rubbing his sore feet. He couldn't remember the last time he'd ever felt such feeble mortal pain.

"May I have a glass of water?"

"Shhh," Sophia hissed. "Our sisters are sleeping."

He glanced around the space, noting the long table near the kitchen with rows of chairs, and the pile of plates stacked atop the counter. He hadn't expected them to be sharing a home, but perhaps at the end of the world, there was some comfort in knowing your coven was together.

"I'll make you a bed on the couch for the night. Tomorrow we will get you settled in," she whispered.

Standing, he stretched his back and followed silently down a narrow hall to a small living room. On the long couch, someone slept, her face buried beneath a heavy blanket. He crossed to the couch he would have called a loveseat and sat, eyeing the long couch enviously.

Sophia pulled a blanket from the chair in the corner and handed it to him. He took it, smiling gratefully, and laid his head down on the arm. It was disorienting after spending so much time in a state of nothingness, followed by the long trek over land to find the last remaining humans, but soon, his eyelids were drifting closed. A tightness in his chest he'd never noticed was gone, lifted for the first time since he had come back from death all those years ago. His thoughts were clear—his own.

A warm hand rested on his shoulder and his eyes fluttered open.

"I'm happy you're here," Sophia said in a soft voice.

He nodded. It had been a long, strange journey to get here, but finally he was home.

CHAPTER 33

Helena

Helena leaned into Aesop, nails digging into his arm as Aniel while Zadkiel held Sanura in place and Michael and Raphael chanted in their strange angelic language. First, they stripped her speed, then her fire magic. Her death magic wasn't so easy. Michael pulled bits and pieces from her one at a time. She screamed as though she were dying.

Helena knew it must be for effect. The man hadn't made a sound; instead he had been almost peaceful as they robbed him of his magic. When Michael took the bit of Sanura's soul that lived in him, he'd sagged as though they'd removed a curse. She couldn't imagine losing her magic, but Peter looked relieved when he opened his eyes.

Pity, he'd been slightly handsome before. Now his dim, unfocused eyes were plain compared to her angel's fiery ones, and his posture was atrocious.

Aniel glanced up, giving her a wry smile.

"It's good your magic can't be stolen, my love. I like your angelic beauty."

He winked as if to say he knew his mate well, but his thoughts were silent as he put all his energy into holding the witch in place while Michael and Raphael continued to work.

When it was done, muted brown eyes glared at them and blunt nails swiped uselessly at the angels holding her upright. They released her and she stumbled forward. Vassi lurched for her, hand outstretched, but the woman darted away as fast as her human legs would carry her.

"Let her go, Witch."

Vassi glanced back at Michael, biting her lip. Coming to some decision, she nodded. Helena could swear Michael had been waiting for her confirmation or approval. His shoulders seemed to sag when she took his hand, squeezing.

Exhaustion weighed on Helena, and she swayed on her feet. In a blink, Aniel was there, lifting her into his arms. She sighed contentedly, leaning close. "I've missed you, soulmate."

He smiled down at her, arms tightening around her. "And I you, my dove. Shall we give the coven a break from your company tonight and sleep under the stars?"

She grinned up at him, but as they stepped through the door into the frigid night, she shivered. "It's too cold."

"Let's go south."

He launched into the sky, not waiting for her response, and hovered just above the tree line as Helena curled into his chest for warmth. She cast a protective bubble around herself to block the wind, sighing as the chill abated. He swept along the canopy, and her eyelids drifted closed.

Helena opened her eyes as they touched down in a meadow some time later. As her feet met the ground, she could feel it was much warmer here, even through the bubble. She let the magic fall away, inhaling the balmy scent.

"It's perfect. Where are we?"

"Mexico."

"Mex-i-co." She sounded out the word. It was warm and lush, seemingly untouched by the war between angels and demons. Helena spun around, taking in the beautiful space, feeling more at home in this forest than she had among the witches in the frigid mountain climate of Colorado. She'd begun to enjoy their company, but something inside her had been frozen in that strange place, around so many who didn't speak her language, and her shoulders relaxed for the first time in the humid warmth of this place. "Can we stay awhile?"

"As long as my dove wishes."

CHAPTER 34

Michael

Vassi tugged Michael toward town and the house he'd taken as his own. She moved fast, deliciously filthy thoughts clouding her mind as she yanked him along.

We are in no rush, Witch.

I owe you thanks for saving my life. Images of her on her knees, doing so much more than thanking him, danced through her mind. His lips twitched. She picked up speed and he went with her, unwilling or unable to deny any longer.

The others had left them, each going their separate way, and though thoughts of his daughter crowded his mind, slicing fresh pain through him, he hoped she might finally find peace now that she was stripped of her vile gift. What he wouldn't give to be rid of it himself.

They reached the door to his home and Vassi twisted the knob. She glanced back, giving him a hungry look. He groaned. She would be the death of him.

Can you die? Her tone was serious and he realized she'd been a silent passenger for that entire inner monologue.

It's rude to listen to my private thoughts.

Is it? You can listen to mine whenever you want. I'm an open book.

Did she know those were the words he needed? That they meant something to his kind? The open vulnerability that came with finding one's mate and knowing your every thought, desire and fear was laid bare for the one who could never deny you.

I do now.

His lip tilted up.

"Is that a smile?"

Michael's mouth fell into a flat line.

"I need to see it again. Give me a smile."

He bared his teeth at her and she spun around, wrapping her arms around him. "You're right. Don't smile. You're more handsome when you're scowling."

A snort escaped him and he pressed his lips firmly together. What was happening to him?

Vassi's mouth stretched into a wide grin. "That was cute."

Cute? Cute! I'm the seraph of death. There's nothing cute about me.

Vassi leaned close, pressing a kiss to his nose. *If you say so.*

Heat burned a path to his chest and his soul strained to be closer, to be touching her everywhere. He gripped her hips, lifting her up and she wrapped her legs around his waist. He walked her backward into one of the home's many bedrooms. She found his mouth, soft lips pressing against his. Where their kisses had been ravenous, almost desperate before, his witch took her time now, exploring his mouth.

Her tentative bites and sucking weren't nervous—she was as confident now as ever, but she enjoyed getting to know him, pressing her body against his as his fingers flexed around her firm ass. He continued down the long hall, tasting her, letting her move against his growing desire.

It had been impractical taking this home when so many were crammed into some of the smaller ones, but he hadn't cared much for the human's plight when he took it. On second thought, why did he care about it now? The witch was corrupting his mind.

He pushed the door wide and pressed her down onto the bed, letting his weight sink into the mattress. His lips left hers, trailing kisses down her neck. She had imagined giving him pleasure, but he could think of so many things he'd rather do to her. His mouth ran over the thin lines bisecting her neck and her hand came up, covering the scars.

He wrapped his fingers around hers, tugging them aside. "These are your battle scars. Don't be ashamed of them."

Vassi's fingers slid over the lines at her neck, tracing a path over her collarbone to the thick white mottled flesh at her chest. She glanced down. "How am I alive?"

Michael sat up giving her room to slide back. He hadn't asked her if she wanted this, hadn't given her a choice. He'd thought only of himself when he brought her back, feeding a part of his soul into her. He traced the outline of the scar. What if she didn't want an eternity tethered to their fucked up trio?

Her lips parted in a silent gasp. "Raphael saved me too?" Her brows crinkled over her nose. "Who is Mary?"

Hearing her name aloud should have been a dagger in his chest. It had been for centuries. A millennium. He let out a slow breath. It hurt, but he could still breathe. Would Raphael feel this pain now when he thought of Vassi? Michael didn't feel the blind rage he'd expected at the thought of another laying claim to her. If it had been anyone else, he would have. It was part of why he'd distanced himself from his twin and their soulmate all these centuries. But now he wasn't sure how Raphael felt.

I don't want your brother. Vassi's hand came up, and she ran a finger along his jaw, tracing the seam of his lips. *Is that okay?*

Some great weight lifted a fraction. She didn't want the perfect twin. She wanted *him*.

Her lips split in a wide grin. "Isn't that what I've been saying?"

Michael fell on her, sucking her lower lip between his and biting. Vassi responded by returning the gesture and their blood, red and gold, mixed in their mouths, tasting of honey and fire and he licked greedily at the lifeforce sustaining them both.

Vassi's arms wrapped around his neck, fingers sliding into his hair and she yanked hard, pulling him closer; they traded essence and spit, finding solace in each other.

Vassi lifted a sweat-slicked cheek from his chest and sat up, frowning. "Why aren't you sweaty?"

"Seraphim do not sweat."

"Unfair."

Michael smiled, rolling onto his side and tracing the row of white lines bisecting her abdomen. *In what battle did you win these scars?*

She glanced down at the X across her stomach, lifting a finger and running it absently over raised flesh. She was silent for a long moment. When Michael raised a hand to touch them again, to hear her thoughts, she opened her mouth and spoke the words aloud.

"My father wasn't a kind man." She looked up, staring past him to the faint rays of sun peeking over the horizon, preparing to illuminate a new day. Michael waited, giving her time to speak her truths. "My mother was a proud, strong witch. My father was always threatened by her, but he never raised a hand to her."

She tucked a cinnamon and bronze strand of hair behind her ear and inhaled a slow breath. "When I was nine, my magic began to manifest. The first time I called water from the sink, he dropped his cup." She blew out a breath, leaning against an arm.

Michael tucked his wing behind his back, watching her in silence. He understood how it felt when others cowered from your gifts. Feared you. Especially those you thought you could rely on.

"The second time, he found me twirling small cyclones over my bowl of cereal." Her gaze darkened. "He demanded I stop. 'Don't play with your food, Vassi. Do it again and you'll get a beating.' They were idle threats. Mama wasn't scared of him and neither was I."

Vassi met his eyes, coldness—bitterness—in her amber gaze. "At least I thought they were. He found me in my room that night; took a bat to my hands while I slept. Mama was out with the coven." Her gaze darkened. "He told me if I told her the truth, the next time she left he'd cut me."

Fire burned in Michael's gut. Hate-filled rage at her father's cruelty, but he said nothing. This sort of pain needed to be released.

"I didn't believe him. When Mama came home, near dawn, I raced for her, raising my mangled fingers and crying out for comfort." She shook her head, eyes dropping from his. "She took me to the healer. They saved my fingers, but my trust was a far more fragile thing. I begged her not to go back there, to face my attacker, but Mama said we didn't back down from a bully."

Michael's jaw popped from grinding it. Another parent who had failed her.

"He wasn't there of course, coward that he was. He'd run. It didn't stop the nightmares." Her fingers were white as they fisted the blankets. "I'd collapsed in my bed after classes, exhausted from so many restless nights when I heard the scrape of my window being pried open."

Michael sat up.

"Blurry-eyed, I took in the dark shape climbing through my window and opened my mouth to scream, but I was too late. A hand clamped down over my mouth. 'I won't let another bitch like your mother loose on the world. You're my problem to solve.' Agonizing pain, that's all

I remember as the dull blade was rammed into my stomach." Vassi's knuckles tightened around the blankets and she sucked in a sharp breath. "But it was worse when he pulled it back out and did it again."

Her free hand flew to the scars on her stomach. "I passed out after that. When I woke, our healer was standing over me, praying I'd live."

She looked up, meeting his eyes again. All the hate and anger from a lifetime of carrying that pain was plain on her face and Michael's shoulders loosened a fraction. This was how they were connected. It wasn't a soul that bonded them, it was the betrayal of those they'd thought they could trust. The ones they were supposed to rely on. The ones they'd been told would always be there for them.

Michael didn't offer her apologies or excuses. He wrapped an arm around her, pulling her to him. She exhaled a shuddering breath and leaned close. Their shared soul glowed, stretching and purring and demanding they mend what was broken in both of them.

Bond with me.

Vassi looked up. *What?*

He searched her face. "Be my soulmate. Spend the rest of eternity with me."

A litany of emotions danced across her face as her mind raced over all the possible implications. Before she answered aloud, he was already smiling.

"Yes."

The End

A THANK YOU GIFT

T hank you so much for completing the Prophecies of Angels and Demons journey with me. To show my appreciation, I'm giving you the first four chapters of the first book in my next series, Deadly Fae Duology, free.

If you loved the characters from the POAAD as much as I did, I have another surprise! One of the characters makes a cameo appearance in Whispers Among Thorns, book one in the DFD.

Reading on your device? Just click the QR code to be redirected.

If you enjoyed Parable, please consider leaving an honest review on your favorite site.

Acknowledgements

I f you've made it this far and kept reading, a special thank-you to you. Readers like you are the reason I love writing.

To my mom, who continues to be my first reader, even the horrible first drafts, I'm so grateful our love of reading brought us even closer.

To my son, who tells everyone he meets about my books, sometimes to my embarrassment. Thank you for being my biggest supporter.

To Brittni, my new alpha reader for reading every crappy draft and still wanting to read the finished book at the end! I love all your comments and emojis. :)

To my street team, for believing in me and being so willing to give your time and energy to share my stories with the world. I hope you got the ending you wanted.

To Michaela Choi for editing an entire series! I bet you didn't think I'd make you read so many books.

And to SCOriginal for all your art pieces.

Thank you.

ABOUT THE AUTHOR

Cassandra Aston grew up near Austin, TX on a ranch just outside the city. She's a lover of everything fantasy, especially the Fae. Although her first series, Prophecies of Angels and Demons, doesn't delve into the realm of the Fae, her next series, Deadly Fae Duology, is a dark portal fantasy that takes the reader deep into the world of Faerie.

She started writing in middle school when her obsession with goosebumps inspired a project that would consume three years of her life and result in over sixty novella length short stories.

When she isn't writing, she's dreaming of far away lands that only exist in a book.

Cassandra lives in Houston, TX with her family of four.

PARABLE

CASSANDRA ASTON
dark fantasy author

Made in the USA
Coppell, TX
18 June 2025

50861108R00100